SHERLOCK HOLMES &
THE SILVER CORD

ALSO BY M. K. WISEMAN

Sherlock Holmes & the Ripper of Whitechapel
Sherlock Holmes & the Singular Affair

Bookminder trilogy:
The Bookminder
The Kithseeker
The Fatewreaker

Magical Intelligence

Forthcoming:
The Poison Game

SHERLOCK HOLMES &
THE SILVER CORD

M. K. WISEMAN

ISBN: 978-1-7344641-6-0 (hardcover)

ISBN: 978-1-7344641-7-7 (paperback)

ISBN: 978-1-7344641-8-4 (ebook)

This is a work of fiction. Any references to real people, places, or historical events are used fictitiously. Other names, characters, places, descriptions, and events are products of the author's imagination or creations of Sir Arthur Conan Doyle and any resemblances to actual places or events or persons, living or dead, is entirely coincidental.

Edited by MeriLyn Oblad

Cover Illustration by Egle Zioma

Interior design created with Vellum

Published in the United States of America

1st edition: August 1, 2023

mkwisemanauthor.com

Contents:

FOREWORD

OR, THE TRUE REICHENBACH:

I watched Watson's receding figure grow small as he picked his way back down the steep path to Meiringen, a doctor's urgency speeding his steps. He looked back twice. When I believed his eyesight unlikely to pick out my form from amongst the jagged boulders at my back, I dismissed the youth who had delivered the message. I needed no guide to Rosenlaui. I was under no illusion I should be allowed to make it there. Of Moriarty's having sent the lad to draw Watson away, I had little doubt. A cold courtesy, but a courtesy nonetheless. Inwardly, I thanked the professor for his foresight and finished the short ascent, keen but not altogether eager for the ending which drew ever nearer.

A note about Reichenbach itself:

The ground around the falls is, in turns, steep and rocky, all of it soaked and slick. The tumbling waters are deafening and relentless. A person sinks into the sound and is drowned even if they do not fall within the water's unforgiving grasp. The mist reaches out further than any man has a right to expect. The spray flies upwards and sideways into the air, a perpetual rain shower—all backed by the noise, noise, noise of the rushing waters. The trees, the grass, bathed in this never-ending mist, grow green and lush all around. Save for what flora has dared reached too close. Such branches hang limp, blackened and bare, flayed alive by the tumbling waters. All cling to those unyielding rocks, their knotted roots holding tight to every crevice and adding to the perilous footing of the place.

The views from the summit, or rather, near the path's ending: exquisite. Rainbows arc in the foaming spray, the shining leaves dance and shimmer, and a person is keenly conscious of their extant indomitab— Nay, of their own fragility. There is, I believe, scarce a more perfect, efficient, and heartless killer than those falls.

Alone, with the mist of the rushing waters gathering great beads on my coat and hat, I waited. It is a strange thing to be balanced between Heaven and Hell, to sit on the lip of a roaring precipice and see grand distant peaks glowing in the afternoon sun, to look down upon pastoral valleys and feel that same stirring in the breast as London gives with its press of buildings and frenetic industry. The world, it holds the same secret yearnings and passions wherever a person may be. Untruths, humbuggery, and blackmail;

peace, love, and honour. Nothing is small, and few things are ever at rest or unchanging. We pick our path, we choose our side, and then everyone else's choices and sides come at us, the good and ill-meaning grappling and altering our lives through their never-ending conflict.

My own conflict would find closure before the day was out. I congratulate myself even now that my guts did not twist at the thought. In imagining the potential outcomes, I had not writhed about, seeking escape, some miracle solution that would condemn my enemy but save myself. I was at peace. The world would be rid of Moriarty. The head would be cut from the snake, and the rest of his terrible organization would fall. The contents of one blue envelope would ensure as much. And Watson—

Here my resolve weakened. I drew forth pen and paper from my pocket. The resulting note has been chronicled elsewhere by its recipient. Heart eased, I rose and flicked my spent cigarette into the alluring, watery void.

But my peace, now scattered, would not easily return to me. I turned, as ever I had, to logic. My actions here and now—my sacrifice—would have meaning. Moriarty, that tricky devil of a man, could not be defeated any other way.

From the corner of my eye, I saw I was no longer alone.

"Mr. Sherlock Holmes," Moriarty said, quickly moving forward along the path so as to position himself between me and any possible escape. Certainly, he knew as well as I that our contest would produce some definite conclusion here and now; the motion, thus, was unnecessary yet not out of character for a man so singularly pledged to malevolence.

"Mr. Moriarty," I answered back, smoothly gesturing with my cigarette case my intention that our interview was not to be rushed. "I presume your use of an ill-disguised messenger means that my having sent Dr. Watson back to Meiringen none the wiser ensures his safety?"

He sneered, and I had my answer. A gentleman's courtesy be damned. Icy water flooded my veins. I had been right from the first. Only one thing would ensure Watson's, Mrs. Hudson's, my brother's safety.

Moriarty rushed at me, and there, on the edge of the falls with its rocky, slick terrain, we grappled. For all that our rivalry had, until today, manifested in words and in the intellectual chess match which had set him so resolutely against me and me against him, our final confrontation remained silent and almost completely physical. He was—as he had ever been—an opponent completely devoid of decency. I found myself pushed to the brink as the professor's desperation found voice in the thrashing of his fists, his fingers becoming wicked talons which I was hard-pressed to avoid. All this I had anticipated, however, and I refused to let go. He had passion and fear and hatred and I . . . I was a blank unfeeling bulwark against which Moriarty could dash himself to pieces! He could claw out my eyes for all I cared. I remained as impassive and unflinching as fact, manoeuvring our conflict to the very edge of the path.

Thus, locked as we were in one another's grasp, I allowed my choice for justice and Moriarty's commitment to evil to propel us both backwards and into empty space. Again, I had anticipated every possibility and prepared myself for this end. He had not. Eyes widening and with a feral growl, he tried to save himself. But it was too late. Moriarty's final words were nothing more than an interminable scream.

I should have died there. There was no scenario wherein I expected life as payment for Moriarty's destruction. And yet rough rock cut into my palms, slippery wet stone which threatened to drop me still uncaringly into the abyss. I now clung to the cliff opposite the lookout whereupon I had awaited Moriarty's pleasure. Somehow, in falling, my hands had found purchase, and be it by length of limb, strength of balance, fate, luck, or a combination of all, I had cheated death.

Or merely delayed its embrace. A glance downward informed me that, yes, Moriarty had succeeded in plunging to his demise and that I should not look down a second time lest it prompt my swift following in his wake. My left

11

foot might find purchase if I stretched. It might—

In reaching out, I glanced up and saw the outline of a man's head and shoulders high above. My hands slipped, and I fell some five feet more. In that same instant, something struck the boulder above me. A loosed shard of stone cut my cheek, and I knew the "something" for what it was: a bullet.

I had sent my second to safety. Moriarty had not.

Without hardly thinking, I threw myself sideways towards a small outcropping which lay out of my pursuer's line of sight and stood as my best chance for giving me time to calculate my route back onto the path above—were there such an option left for me. My coat I bequeathed to the roaring waters. With luck, Moriarty's man would have a glimpse of the item and little more. The afternoon was fading to twilight; my imperfect ruse might buy me reprieve.

I gave myself four minutes to gather my strength. Fifteen minutes later saw me lying exhausted and bloody-handed on another shadowy ledge high above and opposite the path which led back down into Meiringen. Of Moriarty's gunman there was no sign. Uncertainty shook me. For all my careful gathering of evidence, Scotland Yard would have but partial success in dismantling the professor's organization. Life after

Moriarty? There truly was no such thing as life after Moriarty.

And yet here I had it.

Motion on the path to the falls. A handful of men. I shrank further back within the shadows of my hiding spot.

Watson. Watson and several others from the town below. I watched as erroneous yet logical conclusions were made. I saw my dearest companion in all the world read and then reread the note which I had left pinned beneath my cigarette case. I quailed as John's legs seemed to give way under the weight of my words, and he sank down onto a rock, his eyes staring unseeing at the tumble of water that separated us.

At length Watson was drawn off from the fruitless vigil by his companions, and I made ready to emerge from my hiding spot. It was then that my caution rewarded me once more. Moriarty's man, Colonel Moran—my brain helpfully dug the name from my files—stepped from his place of concealment and made to follow the small, sombre contingent back into Meiringen.

Hardened resolve and renewed purpose fuelled my limbs, and I half-climbed, half-scrambled up the cliff face. My motions more than the sound of my ascent drew Moran's attention. It was exactly as I had hoped. The growing gloom of evening was no friend to his marksmanship, and I made it safely back up onto solid ground, whereupon I took off at a run. With my head start and the urgency for survival guiding my steps, I led him on a merry chase through the darkened forest. Eventually it became apparent I had lost my pursuer. Providence wanted me to live, it would seem, though a day and a half later she dropped me penniless, friendless, and half-dead at a little hamlet some ten miles distant of where Moriarty had met his death at my hands.

Eight days and nearly five hundred miles later: Florence. And the semi-reliable safety of my brother's long-reaching connections.

Did I ever look back over my shoulder? Did I ever again hear Moriarty's wild and soul-rending scream? Yes. At every moment, yes. Torn flesh heals. But the mind, the heart? I have yet to find that out.

Take, if you must,
this little bag of dreams;
Unloose the cord,
and they will wrap you round.

— W. B. YEATS

DEAR DIARY

CHAPTER 1

Early morning London is second only to late-night London. In a city never quiet and rarely at rest, there is, daily, a short space of time wherein stillness is grasped at and very nearly realized. In the small hours of the day, the nightmen have come and gone. The labourer rises, refreshed—either from a well-earned slumber or an equally restorative visit to his local public house. The sky, steady and dark, contemplates what hue she will wear today, while the criminal nerve, exposed by this relative peace, falls prey to men such as myself who are so bold or so foolish as to borrow a horse and hansom cab with the plan to spring a trap in the service of justice and the law.

In short, I, Sherlock Holmes, could at present breathe deeply of the pre-dawn air, feeling it all the sweeter, all the clearer, for having now removed one more of the late Professor Moriarty's agents from the freedom of the wider world.

With a wince, I allowed my fingers to dance themselves along the edge of the long scrape which graced the left side of my face and jaw. The grimace was twofold. For one, said injury really hurt. More importantly, I was imagining the consternation with which I would be met upon my arrival at Baker Street. Mrs. Hudson I could dodge until such time as I had managed my medical needs. I had done so on a semi-regular basis in the ten-odd years I had been in residence at 221B. Dr. Watson, however . . . his scolding stood a better chance of hitting home. As well it ought, considering how close to my eye my assailant's attack had landed.

"Watson knows the risks," I groused, reining in the fractious horse. Returning to the yard, I surrendered my cab, tendered my thanks, and offered compliments to the borrowed mare whose steady temper had saved me from a worse beating by my opponent.

From there I walked home through a waking London.

Self-preservation saps curiosity. My dishevelled state painted me the ruffian, and the glances cast my way quickly settled elsewhere lest they draw my attentions. I made it home without incident. An irksome throbbing sprang up in my cheek by the time I let myself into our rented rooms.

Standing before our darkened hearth, I eyed

my desk, contemplating its contents and the delicious insensibility that my needle and morphine bottle could provide. What I craved, however, was a different kind of numbness, the type which provides clarity of mind rather than the suppression of all thought and feeling, though this, too, had its attractions. In the end, an imperfect solution was not a solution, however, and by falling back on practical perseverance, I resisted temptation and found that I was tired. Profoundly bone– and soul-tired. Between couch, chair, and bed, the quickest solution proved the most tempting. I claimed the nearest of the three and, taking care that I stretched myself out on my uninjured side, fell into a dreamless sleep upon 221B's sitting room couch until dawn.

"Good heavens, Holmes."

I awoke to Watson's muttered complaint, and I considered how I must appear to him. The evidence of the prior night's activities clung to my wrinkled clothes, and various bruises on my face and arms had gained new colour during my slumber. More than ever, I was glad that my syringe had remained in its case, though the cut on my cheek screamed at me for having been neglected. It was a wonder I had slept through its anger.

This contrasted with Watson's own tidy-in-dressing-gown-and-slippers domestic self. Without another word, he left my field of vision, returning a moment later with his black bag and a gruff, "May I?"

I sat up. "It's not as bad as it appears—"

"It appears very bad, Holmes." He pulled up a chair opposite me and, frowning, laid out his instruments on the couch. "Goodness! Did you fall from the cab itself?"

"Very nearly," I said simply.

"One of the late Professor's agents?"

"But of course."

He grunted again and allowed silence to grow between us as he dressed the wound on my face. He then seized my right hand, gently turning my wrist so that he might clean and apply a bandage over two split knuckles. I stared, utterly surprised at the colourful collection of bruises and dried blood. An instant later, my brain supplied the answer. I hadn't seen it, because I hadn't wanted to see it. And yet, seeing it now, I could recall the moment and its resulting pain with perfect clarity.

Watson's troubled eyes met mine twice during his brief ministrations. Each time forced a hasty retreat on both our parts. His doctoring was swift and sure. The black bag was taken away and I was bid—again through silence—to arise at my leisure.

I took myself over to the hearth-side cane chair, collecting the previous day's dottles along the way for my morning smoke. A careful pull at my black clay pipe informed me that my wounds would not much trouble me in the coming days. Fine, all fine. I had disturbances enough in the form of a bandaged hand whose damaging I had completely managed to avoid acknowledging.

It appeared I had numbness aplenty after all.

"That's four men now gone from an initial collection of but two," Watson announced from across the room. He rang for coffee and then came to sit opposite me. "Moriarty's enterprise. Legion is thy name."

"My wounds are superficial. The work? Without price."

"Your excusing it is superficial," he grumbled. "And you spend yourself too freely."

I smiled gently at the reproof, far from mollified but unable to admit to it.

It was true enough that I did not lack for work. But neither had I sought celebrity. Returning to life three years after the newspapers have shared far and wide the news of one's death creates stir enough. And besides, Watson was complicit so far as I was concerned. He, too, had upended his life to rejoin me in my work and renew his tenancy at Baker Street.

Our landlady's footsteps sounded on the stair. Without a word, Watson shied yesterday's paper at me, and I quickly adopted an air of aloof distraction behind its pages. I believe a curl of smoke from my morning pipe completed the picture, and Mrs. Hudson ignored me as I ignored her while she set up the implements for breakfast.

The sound of the door clicking shut brought

my *Daily Telegraph*-sponsored privacy screen away from my face.

"Come have some coffee, Holmes," Watson offered, "and you can tell me all about how this latest foe fell."

I sat and poured myself a cup, thinking of the leering face, of the curious weightless sensation I had noted as I hung perilously from the top of my borrowed cab. Moriarty's agent. How many more might spring up in his wake? None. If I had done my research as accurately as hoped. This was the end of it. I had come away with but a scratch and nothing more. I reached for the accumulation of correspondence which sat beside my plate, seeing nothing save for the bandage on my hand.

A scratch and nothing more . . . I shook off the foreboding, the secret shame that I should have come away from that contest with so little in the way of penance. I said, "You recall the garroter Parker?"

Watson shook his head.

"He watched our rooms this past April when looking out for my return on the morning of the incident with Colonel Moran. In the excitement of apprehending the colonel with our little trap, I lost track of Parker. Until last week, that is. And I really do believe, old man, that he is the final consequential member of Moriarty's gang to lose his liberty."

Eyeing me all the more closely, Watson

frowned and said, "You ought to have taken me into your confidence on this one."

I waved off the concern. "I was more in peril from my choice of perch and conveyance than from that villain's wire. But—oh, ho! What is this now?"

The ringing of the doorbell saved me from further flimsy assurances. Youthful footsteps below informed us that our page had gone to meet whoever stood upon our doorstep. Said footsteps sounded again, more composed and accompanied by the light step of the individual who had come to call.

Watson and I exchanged a quick look, and each of us dove into hasty preparations. He had been far more ready for the day than I and so received our visitor while I retreated to my room to make myself minimally presentable. I returned moments later to find the doctor sitting on our couch in animated conversation with a woman.

Dressed in the latest fashion, though not ostentatiously, she was what Watson would term "handsome." I estimated her age to be approximately fifty, and she appeared to be recently recovered from some serious illness. Widowed. Possessing independent means. Labouring beneath the polite pleasantries exchanged with Watson, the twin monsters of worry and despair warred for dominance.

"Mr. Holmes!" Seeing me, the woman jumped to her feet, but she quickly recovered her poise.

"My apologies, Mr. Holmes. Your friend here has been ever so kind to me and all without knowing the nature of my problem. For I truly do not know where to begin other than to say that my life is over and my reputation nearing irreversible ruin."

Trembling, she held out a crisp piece of stationery which had been folded into quarters. She said, "You'll find the extent of my troubles right there on that page. I am Margaret. And Percy—"

She sank listlessly back onto the couch, her gaze lowered. "And the other would be Mr. Percy Simmons, friend of my late husband."

Habit took over, and I returned to the well-trod paths of thought and observation, picking up excitement and inspiration along the way as my eyes took in the contents of the paper. A strong feminine hand had penned the words, and the prose style was akin to what one might find in a diary. The scene, if it might be described thus, began in the middle. In the middle of a sentence, to be precise. The incomplete account opened with our two paramours in an indecorous position and left them in the midst of expressing ardent affections for each other.

Impassively, I handed back the page and waited.

Our visitor took a shuddering breath and began, "I cannot account for this paper, Mr. Holmes. It is the third such one that I have received in as many months. I have no memory of its composition, though there is no mistaking that it is my handwriting. And there is some small truth to what you have read there on the page, though I would never have phrased it so indecently. My husband was the late Mr. Cyril Jones who you may have encountered during one of your prior cases due to his position within our government. No? A pity. His reputation would have provided the endorsement I fear I shall need. Let me be perfectly clear that I loved my husband, and he was the best of men."

A short, hiccupping gasp interrupted Mrs. Jones' fervent appeal, and she stopped to compose herself. She continued, "As I say, there is truth at the heart of this blackmail. For blackmail it must be, Mr. Holmes."

I raised my eyebrows at the insistence. "We have no such assurances. It could well be a bene-factor trying to save your reputation, having come upon these pages through some means or another. This paper. It arrived within an envelope?"

"I had not thought to keep it. For me, the contents were of such value as to render the casing irrelevant."

"The date posted. The location. The hand of they who posted said note to you. All might have been of some assistance." I frowned. "Your current fortunes. How much depends upon no scandal from before your husband's passing becoming public knowledge?"

"My husband was a successful man who made

certain that I did not want. But my inheritances are my own." She smiled archly. "There are no others who could step forward with a claim were my reputation or my loyalty to my husband during his lifetime called into question. My finances are unencumbered from such antiquated restrictions."

"This Mr. Simmons, then. Take me back to the beginning."

Mrs. Jones swallowed self-consciously and began what felt like a well-rehearsed set of facts. "My late husband had amongst his associates a man named Percy Simmons with whom, early in his career, he developed the most intimate friendship. I am not aware of the circumstances by which they made acquaintance. Their friendship was merely a fixture in Cyril's life. Throughout our engagement and my marriage to Mr. Jones, Mr. Simmons became to us something akin to family. His presence has been a comfort to me in the years since my husband's passing."

"And the truth of your relationship to Mr. Simmons?" My eyes flicked to the paper in Mrs. Jones' hand.

"It happened some ten years back. My husband never knew of the brief indiscretion in which Percy and I indulged." She blushed. "A moment of weakness and nothing more, but I have regretted it all my days since. That which is written on the page there? It is a gloating account; a bit of pretty prose unworthy of even the most lewd novelist. I would never! Again, I swear to you, on all I hold dear, that I did not write those words, Mr. Holmes."

"And yet," I mused, "Someone has worked very hard to make it appear as though you have."

"You believe me then, Mr. Holmes?" Relief sparked tears in the corner of Mrs. Jones' eyes. "Oh, thank the heavens! I had half feared you would tell me I was delirious and show me to the door. I have been at my wit's end wondering over it."

Flashing a quick smile, I turned and seated myself in the chair opposite. "And so tell me, Mrs. Jones, how such a paper has come into your possession. For, clearly, the story of its provenance is as enthralling as its contents, yes?"

"Late this past spring, I received in the post a warning. A brief unsigned letter was sent to me stating that evidence of my misdeeds had fallen into the hands of a party bent on my destruction, and the cost for protection would be my silence."

"Silence is a fairly modest extortion," I observed. "There were no demands made alongside the threat?"

"No, Mr. Holmes." She shook her head. "And so I burned the letter. It scared me to even possess the threat. I had foolish hopes that that would be the end of it, but a week later, the first page of this . . . sordid account, arrived at my door. I recall that it began quite innocently—some small observations about the weather and a dress I had been contemplating—before moving on to less virtuous musings. I was struck both by the oddity of it and the implied menace. A diary entry in my handwriting, written as if they were my thoughts put down on the page for safekeeping, but of which I had no memory.

"I ran to my desk and found that, no, there appeared to be nothing missing or added. My diaries were intact and undisturbed. Three and a half weeks later, a second page was sent. You have seen the third, which I received two days ago. It is, so far, a fairly straightforward narrative and styled, as I say, to match my personal writings."

"Have you the other two pages?"

"I burned each the very day that I received them."

"Tsk, tsk, Mrs. Jones."

"I panicked! The evidence seemed damning, and I hadn't the faintest idea of who was threatening me."

"Or why," Watson chimed in.

I remained in quiet contemplation for a moment, and then, "The dress."

"Beg pardon?"

"The dress described on the now-burned page one of the mysterious manuscript. Do you remember it? Was it true? The weather being observed, can you recall it with particular clarity or confirm its accuracy?"

She blinked in surprise. "I . . . How strange. The dress I remember but not because I had intended on having such a one. It was a colour I coveted and nothing more. It wouldn't have suited my complexion and maturity, you understand. It was more akin to an echo of an old memory. An obsolete girlish hope given voice—as is often the case with diary entries, you understand. I had not given it much thought when I read the mysterious page, as it was not the portion of the text to cause me alarm. As for the weather, one fine day is indistinguishable from the next, and what was described there was appropriate to the season and year that the diary entry purported to be from. So, to your question, yes. The rest of these private observations are as factual as that which you have read there."

"Thank you, Mrs. Jones," I murmured. "And this Mr. Simmons, are you still in regular contact with him?"

"Socially, Mr. Holmes," came her curt reply. Her face closed itself to me.

I rose. "I admit there is very little to go on, what with three-quarters of the evidence having been disposed of. I will take the case, of course. There is, however, the question of the page which you now possess."

Indecision rippled through our client's face, and she unearthed the offending missive once more. "You have my trust, Mr. Holmes, though it pains me to know this has left my safekeeping."

"Blackmail, Mrs. Jones, is a crime for which I harbour a particular repugnance," I assured her.

"No eyes save for my own will read this or any other pages you wish to entrust to my care."

Mrs. Jones looked to Watson and blushed. "My apologies to you. I— I just cannot help but fear— Surely you understand."

"There, there," he soothed. "I am partner to Holmes' work only so far as I am needed, and there is no man more worthy of your confidence than he. He will get to the bottom of this mystery, and the unseen enemy who harasses you shall be stopped."

With tears in her eyes, Mrs. Jones thanked us both and stood to leave. "If I hear anything, anything at all, I will come to you."

"No more fireplaces."

"No, no fireplaces nor candles," she laughed. "And if it would be useful, I could send to you some samples of my usual writing. Nothing so exciting as is written there, but if what I have given you just now is a clever forgery, perhaps it would help to see what I authentically claim as my own?"

"Indeed, Mrs. Jones. At your earliest convenience." With that, we bid her good day, promising we would be in touch as I learned more about her case.

The door closed behind her. I eyed Watson with some bemusement. "Well, Mrs. Jones is in an interesting situation, is she not? A whole sordid tale, penned in her hand, sent to her doorstep by

—an enemy? a champion of her and Simmons' honour?—and she 'cannot account for it.' "

"She's lying, clearly."

"Or . . . ?"

My question was met with the blank stare of frustration.

"Or, she cannot account for it," I answered for him, sitting myself back at our table to enjoy my now-cooled breakfast. "Come now, Watson, surely you do not need to know the exact contents of that page?"

Peevish, he had taken himself over to the bookshelf. "It would be ungentlemanly of me to press. My argument is in your limiting my involvement, particularly when you know how I feel about your over-engaging yourself of late. Here, the entry for forgers."

"Thank you, Watson." Accepting the index from him, I settled into my chair. And thus our morning passed in quiet, familiar companionship, he with his breakfast and bitter annoyance and me blissfully oblivious inside my intellectual pursuits.

"HE IS EVIL"

CHAPTER 2

Sweeping up the detritus of Professor Moriarty's gang occupied but a fraction of my energies in recent days. The case I built against the operation three years prior had been solid, and the police had done their part. The pieces left upon the board were but minor players and of no threat to me and mine. Petty crime and pettier criminals. Well, petty knife-bearing criminals with decent left crosses. What remained was my own reluctance to be done with it.

My injuries were fairly healed by the time the ruffian who had given me said wounds stood trial two weeks later and was found guilty on all charges. Thus had evaporated my last bastion of defence against the teeming masses who crossed the threshold of Baker Street at every waking hour and wrote requesting assistance during all the other times of the day. Word of my return had long made its circuit, of course, and while one might have thought that this news meant for a quieting of crime, the mere presence in London of one Sherlock Holmes, consulting detective, had quite the opposite effect.

There was, of course, the Mrs. Jones black-mailing case. She had sent me samples of both correspondence and private writings, prompting me to cool my efforts in trailing the current where-abouts of the less talented of forgers in my list. If it were not our client who had penned the damning pages of our case, someone singularly gifted in fakery was fabricating the whole of it.

I was in regular communication with Mr. Edward Maunde Thompson, principal librarian of the British Museum, on a matter that managed to be simultaneously bizarre and whimsical. This while my brains were enmeshed in a delicate little Colombian affair—the details of which I may someday permit Watson to chronicle, should my brother allow light to be shed upon such deep political manoeuvrings. Inspectors Gregson and Lestrade seemed to be taking turns at annoying me. There were social visits; unexpected and uncomfortable travels. False noses and falser wigs. Puzzles and clues. Delicious dead ends which kept me from my couch for days on end. I had again eyed my little velvet case, locked in my desk drawer, but never had occasion or need for its use. Very few were turned away from our doorstep; nearly no telegrams went unanswered. Advertisements to the agony columns of various newspapers were so numerous as to run a charge to equal half of Watson's army pension—had the accolades of successful cases not been able to pay for such expenses tenfold, of course. My Irregulars, sadly, had all been granted a long holiday lest their youthful faces become overly familiar in certain quarters due to how often they were employed in this intrigue and that.

I was, in a word, busy.

Three years abroad and unable to lay claim to my own name had crystallized a new passion within me. More than ever, I was my work. For in work my intellect remained occupied, distracted by its service to the common good. Whatever that might mean.

And so I ran without running, lest I have to stop and consider who I was and why. And it was under Watson's ever-solicitous gaze and kindly guidance that I managed to remember to eat, to sleep, and to amuse myself in ways that reminded myself I was man and not a mere mind.

Tonight stood as excellent example of the direction my companion provided. Watson had suggested dinner and a concert. Dr. Richter was conducting a series at St. James's Hall. Two Wagner pieces were listed in the day's programme, and while I did not believe my brain required the respite, I will admit that I dressed with an eagerness which surprised me.

All through my preparations I concocted and

rehearsed a series of increasingly inane excuses to give to Watson as reason for begging off on our plans. None found utterance, of course. He knew my calendar, its demands, to a greater degree, and I knew better than to claim any sort of sudden malady around the dear doctor. But this, this was what happened if I stopped thinking.

Rather, this was what happened if I allowed my thoughts free rein at all.

Normalcy, frank normalcy, was now as foreign to me as the surface of the moon. I had been home for over five months. Yet I still slept with one eye open—when I slept. I hurried through a simple meal—when I ate. I have never been a nervous man. And yet I found that I searched the faces of strangers with a keenness which told me I yet awaited . . . something. My accursed sense of self-preservation prevented me from considering what that might be.

We left our apartment and, arm in arm, made for Simpson's. Watson and I had barely rounded the corner when, slowing our steps, I said, "A return home?"

"Why, Holmes, whatever is—? Ah, the man there. Yes."

Watson, too, had now spotted the umbrella peddler coming out to hawk his wares. The first fat spatters of rain begin to fall as we strode back onto our street.

Our return errand was to benefit us twofold. A gentleman stood before the door of 221B. I surmised that he had not yet rung, for in the changing weather Mrs. Hudson would have been sure to answer swiftly. Besides that, our potential client's dithering footsteps and furrowed brow spoke of indecision. His hat he had clutched in his hand, the brim crumpling to ruin under nervous fingers.

The man watched as Watson and I approached, never himself moving far from his place of sentry. His dress and the intelligence upon his worried face told me that our visitor was well off and of a position in life that had kept him unused to whatever turmoil had now sent him to pace our doorstep.

"I can call again, Mr. Holmes, Mr. Watson," he began, stepping back and then starting forward just as abruptly. "I see now that I have picked a bad time."

"Not at all." Watson smiled broadly. "Our timing may be quite perfect, as I see you are without an umbrella, and we were returning to fetch one ourselves. Do come inside and tell us the reasons for your coming to see Mr. Holmes and me. Perhaps we may weather out this unexpected rain shower and save ourselves an inclement walk before the dinner hour."

Blinking, the man looked about him as if noting the coming rain for the first time. "Inside. Yes. That would be prudent."

Our visitor's distracted air hung about him like a fog as we ascended the stairs. His shoulders slumped beneath an invisible weight, rendering the otherwise aristocratic man as wilted as his maltreated hat. Something was crushing his spirit. The makings of a case, of course. An interesting one? We should soon see.

As I have said, at present I was taking on all problems that arrived at my door, save for the extraordinarily mundane or those with whom I harboured a moral objection. Watson would say I was working too hard, though he was wise enough not to.

"Please do have a seat," Watson offered our guest.

A fleeting smile of acknowledgment graced his lips, but our visitor remained standing. "If I may? I fear I shall lose my nerve if I so much as move."

"By all means," I said and seated myself so that I could listen with half-closed eyes.

After an accommodating pause, our visitor began, "My name, gentlemen, is Mr. Percy Simmons."

I sat forward in the chair, attentive.

The Mr. Percy Simmons, of Mrs. Jones' diary entries fame?

Interesting indeed.

Good old Watson allowed nary a flicker of recognition to cross his face, though I saw he was quick to draw forth pen and paper and adopt his own posture of keen concentration.

"I am a—" Mr. Simmons paused, cocking his head to the side wistfully. He asked, "I presume that, in the disclosure of my case, there is little chance of my hiding from you my profession?"

"If it is pertinent, I should know of it. You are a barrister if I am not mistaken?"

"That is true, yes. My goodness, Mr. Holmes, you are as perceptive as they say." He blinked in surprise. "I suppose I ought not have named that which fills the other half of my life a profession, per se. It is a calling. A deep and wonderful responsibility. Are you, by any chance, familiar with a group known as the Theosophical Order of Odic Forces?"

I was not. A glance to Watson told me he hadn't any familiarity with the group, either.

"I should hope you haven't, else my own reluctance to speak would have rendered me a fool. Our order is a secret one. For the safety of our brethren and for the safety of society at large, we keep our knowledge hidden from the public.

"I speak of magic, Mr. Holmes. And it is through magic that my friend, Mr. Winter, has been spirited off. It is through magic that he has been assaulted by our enemy." Simmons smiled sadly. "And now you are to show me out. I will return to the side of my friend and regret my disclosure of secrets over which I was honour bound to keep silent. There I will wait for Mr. Winter's essence to die out and for the enemy amongst our ranks to come and finish me as well."

"What is the nature of Mr. Winter's affliction? Understanding, of course, that my colleague and I know next to nothing of your order's practices," I prompted. "You intimate that a definite attack has taken place. Surely there are others more versed in your beliefs, someone who might be of more use than Dr. Watson and me?"

"I am responsible for the man's safety! He is my novice! He has sent his double away under my encouragement!" Shaking and goaded into candour, with voice raised and eyes wild, Mr. Simmons had lost his strange, floaty disconnect. He continued, softer, but no less intense, "Mr. Winter does not eat; he does not drink. He is the third of our sect to fall this way within the past twelve months. He lies as one dead but is clearly not, and I cannot—dare not—tell anyone. I am responsible. It is a tragedy connected with my order, and it is on me to ensure that our powers are unabused."

"Has he any household staff? Anyone attending him?"

"An elderly cousin. And she has no notion of the enemy who presses us nor the true nature of Mr. Winter's affliction. He has lain thus for nine days."

"How is it you have waited until the third victim to seek help? What did the police conclude for the others?"

"They concluded nothing. What could they have?" Despair coloured Simmons' response. "The police looked into the deaths as a matter of course, but there are no suspects when there is no suspicion or even any apparent connection between two very different tragedies. Sorcery, such as that which my friend Winters has attempted, is a dangerous thing. When the soul has gone wandering, the body lies vulnerable."

We waited while Simmons paused to order his mind.

"I hadn't considered foul play with the other victims as they were—" Our guest smiled crookedly. "The others were, shall we say, less adept than someone of Winter's grade. It is only now, in hindsight, that I see the pattern begin to emerge, God help me. If I could tell a person anything about this, if I dared disclose my membership in the Order to anyone save yourselves, I might have chosen to go back to the police and beg that they look closer. But what is it they would see? Nothing. This enemy leaves no trace, no evidence."

"Save for the state of this current victim, Winter."

"Yes, Winter." Simmons nodded enthusiastic, fervent agreement. "We might yet save him. Or, if I should fail, learn something from this latest tragedy, a crime by an unseen hand and leaving no mark. Our adversary, he must be a magician like myself, like Winter. Must be. I feel him. I know him to be there. Working through attacks as invisible as wind but whose effects are just as noteworthy as when the gale is strong enough.

"When a magician chooses to use his powers

for ill . . ." Simmons shuddered. "He is evil, Mr. Holmes. He is evil, and the world itself does not acknowledge his presence, his terrible actions. You observe that neither you nor Dr. Watson know anything that might help me with my problem, knowing nothing—and, I can see from your faces, believing nothing—of magic. But I say you are the right men. Having followed your career, noted your accomplishments. You know justice. You understand evil. And that is enough to gain my complete confidence and faith. Help me, Mr. Holmes. I seek to stop a person who is more than a mere criminal. They are an affront to virtue itself."

Through Simmons' impassioned speech, I had felt the room stretching around me. Watson, this self-proclaimed magician of Odic Forces, each sat small and impossibly distant. A chasm had opened up within 221B. And from that chasm had poured forth all the questions I had thus far managed to avoid. Questions of good and bad and a person's right to lay claim to any system of morality. I understood evil? Which side of it was I meant to understand?

Like the very argument from which I ran, the path I traced in my mind was circular. Our sitting room became a labyrinth wherein, by seeking escape, I ended up running towards the very thing I was trying to flee. And yet, viewed from this angle, viewed through the lens of Simmons' words and rock-strong beliefs, my bitter cynicism looked different. In my curiosity, I lost my grip on the anger and contempt I held for myself.

And then I was back in my chair, by the fire, with the room returned to its normal comfortable proportions. Would that I felt so calm and natural inside. Inside I quaked still, my mind vibrating with interest like a harp string plucked by a skilful musician. I rose, smiling gently as I showed Mr. Simmons out and voiced my usual promises.

As I say, I was at present accepting any and all cases for which I held no outright moral objection. I was intrigued. I was repulsed. I was incredulous. And I was absolutely going to take this case.

GOOD OLD-FASHIONED CHARLATANISM

CHAPTER 3

"For the fun of it, Watson! Besides the curious connection to Mrs. Jones, surely you wish to see what logical explanation Mr. Simmons' tale may have at its conclusion?"

We had resumed our walk to dinner having ended our interview and made an appointment to visit the insensible Mr. Winter on the morrow. The brief rain shower had long passed, rendering our umbrellas superfluous, but the strange interlude at 221 had dampened my companion's spirits. His measured step was sombre and sullen.

"You know better than to ask me that, Holmes. For you know that I would prefer you spend your energies on worthier topics. Or, more importantly, on rest. A blackmailer who doesn't blackmail and an errant sorcerer? Posh." He shook his head.

"Is not dinner out and a Richter concert leisure enough for you?"

"You know what I mean, Holmes."

In all actuality, I hadn't. And it had long been a point of perpetual friction between us. My ideas of what my body and mind could tolerate pitted against his physician's sense and standards. Watson knew when to push me and when to let me be, that self-same friction sometimes finding its source in the fact that I did not often extend him that same courtesy. I said, "I will find your input invaluable on this one, old man."

"What is it you suspect?"

"Besides good old-fashioned charlatanism?" I laughed, then sobered. "Poison is not unlikely. Questioning Mr. Winter may go a long way in determining the borders of fact and fancy. That is, if we are able to rouse him."

"If your suspicions are correct—that he may be a victim of long-term poisoning—we ought to have gone out to see the man straight away." Watson shook his head.

"Now which of us is suggesting we abandon leisure for the drudgery of work at all hours and in all corners?"

"That is unfair, Holmes."

We walked in silence for some distance before I answered the unspoken charges that Watson had levelled at me. "Poison is a reasonable explanation, yes. As is humbuggery on a grand scale. But Simmons' words hold weight, too. His words and the delivery thereof."

"So you are willing to entertain his wild notions." Watson groaned. "I had half a worry that might be the case."

I set my jaw to the reproof. It was my own fault that he had said it, after all. I considered how I might explain myself. "Poison is common. Murder, pedestrian. Arson. Kidnapping. Highway robbery. The methods, means, and motives with which they are carried out are the only elements providing any variety. But what if, Watson, there is more available for a criminal's bag than a knife or a rope? What if a safe may be cracked or a household burgled by something more elegant and rare than the vulgar jemmy and lockpick? What if a crime may be committed leaving no evidence save for what the soul can sense?"

"I do believe you are wearing my hat, Holmes." Watson allowed himself to smile, if grimly. "Typically it is I following the magician about in hopes of determining how it is he has done his tricks. Far be it from me, though, to work at odds to both you and your clients. You know that I am your man until the end."

We turned our talk to lighter things during dinner, my mind roaring all the while. Mr. Simmons' words continued to haunt me in ways I could not have described. A door had been opened. Wordless ideas conceived and hopes indulged, if only for an instant. And now I couldn't unthink and unhope. Taking this case? That was me, actively choosing to prop that door open, to lean on hope, to entertain the glamour and attraction of a belief in a power outside the self.

There was, as I had said, the problematic intersection with the Jones case. But even Watson could see through that excuse. The truth of the matter was that my imagination had been sounded. I could not help but feel myself caught up by this latest puzzle. A dissected puzzle for which I had no pieces, no details save for this strange, keening interest inside.

I do believe I made for a terrible dining companion, but I was too distracted to notice.

Wagner has in his compositions the innate ability to carry the listener through any number of emotional landscapes within scant minutes' time that rarely, if ever, tips over into melodrama. With my conscience and imagination being somewhat raw from their exertions, I was ready for symphonic solace. There amongst the audience at St. James's Hall, I found my balm for both body and mind. I could admit to it that Simmons' words had stirred more than my intellect. His talk of evil had disquieted me. He had spoken of evil with as much conviction and surety as ever I had heard and then charged me with its knowledge.

I had confronted so-called evil in my many hundreds of cases. But could I name it? Dare I define the malevolence which I had hunted so diligently? I could not. Even having risked my life in service to the so-called good.

Practically speaking, what I had said to Watson was true. This case would most likely grant me access into an arena in which few were allowed entrance. I might learn something of use whilst I surveyed this new unmapped section of London, the aetherous realm of magic. Or at least I had before me a set of unknown, and likely well-connected, practitioners who believed in and trod those airy corridors with their arcane practices. It was new society, or a new side of Society.

Or it was base poison, and Mr. Simmons was victim to his own senses and I a fool. In which event my involvement had its ordinary merits and might work in the service of solving Mrs. Jones' puzzling case of anti-blackmail.

No, Holmes, no.

I could pretend to practicality. I could think and reason and have a mystery concluded at the end of the day. But the attraction of this case . . . Evil. Good. Justice. Crime. Power. These were concepts which I had long taken as fact. Presumed facts which begged questions I had never wrestled with. And yet, the answers? They might well be my soul's defence to every action I had ever undertaken in the service of my unique profession.

I glanced to Watson, noting his wistful, relaxed attitude as the concert droned on around us.

Steady Watson. Dependable and true and, in his own way, another answer. Possibly the answer. For why else had I returned? Who else in my life had held any sway with me? I speak in terms of people, not precepts here. I had had my holiday. I had enjoyed three years without a single thread binding me to this or that place, any one responsibility save for my own to myself and the finishing of what I had begun with Professor Moriarty. A task which ought to have ended neatly and without any loose ends at the edge of a cliff outside of Meiringen. But to close the entry on Moriarty was to bury my own acknowledgement that I had been cavalier with my own life and with Watson's.

This, and every other guilt, had arisen in me at Simmons' call.

What Watson did not understand—what I could never tell him, for it would mean my having to say it aloud, to admit it at all—was that my work served to keep me from that terrible precipice of fear which lived at the heart of cold logic. Fear which Mr. Simmons had sounded alongside every other sin of mine when he stood in the doorway of our sitting room and proclaimed that I knew justice, that I understood evil.

Wrong on both counts, Mr. Simmons.

But if I could learn its contours, if there was a

systematic proof, a morality to be gleaned from data and fact? Then this case which he had presented to me had the power to solve my ideological dilemma, that of evil. A question which had haunted me every waking day since Moriarty's demise at my hands.

A HOUSE CALL

CHAPTER 4

We returned to Baker Street to find an answer to the note I had sent to Mrs. Jones. We were to call upon her in the morning before continuing on to our next appointment with Mr. Simmons. That is, provided she harboured no objection to us taking his case in addition to her own.

Watson bid me a good evening, and left to my own devices, I spent my late night and early morning reading in pursuit of all things mystic. I hadn't much applicable in my books readily to hand, but it was a start and something for my questing brain to catch on lest in my restlessness I fall to less productive activities. Watson slept. As the time for our appointment with Mrs. Jones neared, I reluctantly broke off my reading to consult the train schedule. Quick morning ablutions and we were away.

Mrs. Jones resided at Number 26 Hill Street. Settled amongst other well-to-do, respectable neighbours, hers was befitting a woman of her station in life. However, the lady of the house herself answered the door to our ring.

"I have just sent Judy out," she explained, ushering us in. "We may speak as candidly as we like."

"I trust there have been no further communications?" I asked, wondering how often Mrs. Jones orchestrated having her house alone to herself. It certainly enabled private discussions or private doings.

She smiled, colouring slightly. "No letters save your own from yesterday evening, Mr. Holmes. Do come sit down."

We did as we were bid, and in the awkward pause which followed, Mrs. Jones offered, "I do believe I have recalled one thing about the letters which I had burned. You had mentioned that the envelopes would have been useful to you for the evidence they bore. Upon further reflection, I am absolutely certain that none of them had the same postmark. All London, but none from here. It added to the mystery, the menace of it, as I could only imagine for myself some individual sneaking about to post these letters. An attack all the more personal for its impersonality."

"They might simply have dropped the packet in any letter box in any corner of the city."

Horror crossed Mrs. Jones face. "Oh, to think

these pages could have passed through so many hands."

"There, there, Mrs. Jones," Watson soothed. "Whoever sent them to you wanted them in your safekeeping."

I set my jaw to the kind assurance. While Watson's observation was literally true, the unknown menace remained. A threat had preceded these postings, and while it was a relief to Mrs. Jones to have these pages in hand, there remained the question of how many more were in the hands of the mysterious sender and what they intended to do with them. I could surmise, from the sample of the one page, that the trajectory of its contents was towards the provocative. If the mere mention of a postal letter box sparked fear within our client's face, months of trepidation in opening one's mail seemed a cruel enough torture.

The consideration had me careful in my next choice of words. My overnight reading had furthered my initial suspicions regarding the gentleman who had called upon us yesterday. The Post Office Directory for the current year had a half a column dedicated to folk of the name of Simmons. There was but one who was a Percy. I asked, "I have a question for you, Mrs. Jones, which may seem both indelicate and insensitive. Your friend Mr. Simmons. Have you any idea of whether he is acquainted with a man by the name of Winter?"

"Oh!" Mrs. Jones' hands fluttered to her

mouth. "So he has been to see you about poor Mr. Winter. I ought to have realized."

"Mr. Simmons coming by yesterday is what prompted my telegram to you, yes," I said. "Your candidness puts me at ease, for I had some reservations on how you might react to my taking a case of his, considering where I stand with your own. Neither Watson or myself will disclose that we are handling your delicate little matter, of course, but your reaction tells me that you've some inkling of Mr. Winter's state and, very likely, have had a hand in Mr. Simmons gracing our doorstep yesterday evening."

"That is true, Mr. Holmes. I mentioned you to Mr. Simmons three days ago. In addition to having been a close friend to my husband, as well as myself"—Mrs. Jones' blush renewed itself—"he has this knack for putting one's heart at ease on all things spiritual. His education is quite remarkable."

"Know you the nature of Mr. Winter's affliction?" Watson pressed as delicately as a train engine. I blanched. If we could not be entrusted to keep Simmons' case to ourselves, how might Mrs. Jones believe our discretion on her matter?

She pursed her lips. "He has told you of his theosophists."

"He entrusted that information to us, yes," I conceded.

"As I sent him your way when he told me of

their most recent troubles, I cannot fault your edging along the lines of what you can and cannot admit to," she said. "Personally, I believe in the Order's tenets. You are not unveiling any new thing about Percy's life to me."

"And are you a practitioner yourself?" Watson asked.

"The Theosophic Order of Odic Forces is only open to men." The bitter note in Mrs. Jones' voice was unmistakable.

"Then you have no objection to our taking on Mr. Simmons' case?"

"None whatsoever." Mrs. Jones smiled. "I thank you for your thoughtful concerns."

Having gained the street and commenced making our way onward to Charing Cross Station, Watson turned to me and said, "So, to her mind, the cases are not connected."

"To the evidence we have at present, no, the cases are not connected. Only inconveniently linked," I said, my thoughts turned steadfastly inward.

Our walk was short but not so short as to prevent me from catching my partner up on the fruits of my hasty research from the hours before. A few snatches of rumour, a smattering of facts—mainly the who and the where and the when of certain organizations—were all that I had been able to glean from my catalogue of clippings. London had, at present, no less than half a dozen sects which dedicated themselves to the study and practice of magic. Their names, their member-ships, were as guarded as the secret knowledge they professed. Mr. Simmons had risked much in even approaching us with what vague details as he had disclosed.

"Standard! Who's for the Standard? Times here! Morning papers! Paper, gentlemen! Who's for the Standard? Times! Times! Mo-orning papers!"

The familiar cry of the newspaper boy drew us out of our conversation, and we availed ourselves of his wares. Obtaining sustenance in the form of coffee and Banbury cakes—Watson was hungry, I merely indulgent—we made our way towards the ticket counter. It was at this point that I purchased one ticket and handed it over to Watson.

"Meet me back at Baker Street once you've met with Simmons and seen to Winter, and tell me all that you learn."

"What?" Watson ejaculated.

"We have tested Mrs. Jones, now we shall test Simmons. You are more than capable of acting in my stead."

"And what should I tell Simmons?"

"Tell him . . . tell him the truth. Tell him I have been overworking myself, wearing myself thin day and night and have now discovered that I need the morning if I am to be any use to anyone at all."

"He came upon us as we were going out last night," Watson grumbled.

"Goodbye, Watson. You have my complete trust in this matter." I waved him off and allowed the crowd to close 'round me.

I really did rest upon my return to Baker Street. How quickly I returned there for said rest is another matter entirely. For I truly was as busy as I had just then claimed. I had a visit to Scotland Yard which I had been putting off. There was the British Museum quandary. The activities of two forgers needed looking into—unrelated to the Jones case. These errands and others I quickly attended to. Plumstead was not all that far a destination, and I hadn't the faintest idea of what Watson might truly be called upon to do with regards to attending to Mr. Winter. Poison was still the lead consideration. The doctor's examination might not be lengthy.

In the end, I returned home before my colleague and thus finally managed the idleness which had long evaded me. Watson found me laid out upon the couch, pipe in hand and newspaper strewn across my lap.

"Well, that was an interesting interlude," he proclaimed.

"Mr. Winter?"

"Fine, fine. Malnourished and completely ill from his misadventure in the great unknown but I anticipate a full recovery. No poison." This he said with a sly sideways glance towards me.

I sat up, folded my legs beneath me, and very calmly relit my pipe.

Watson sat himself down, drew forth cigarette and match, and indulging in the one for several long minutes, began his report:

"I enjoyed a quiet and uneventful train ride following your abrupt abandonment at Charing Cross. You retained the *Standard*. Here is the *Times*. You'll find something for you in the advertiser's section, I believe." Watson leaned forward to toss the *Times* atop the growing stack at my side. "But that is for another case. Simmons' troubles have the chance of becoming legitimately interesting.

"I alighted in Plumstead, whereupon Mr. Simmons met me at the station. I gave your regrets, and he and I proceeded on foot to Mr. Winter's house. Winter lives not far from the station. On our walk, Simmons filled me in on some more details regarding his friend. I am told he worked as a secretary for Jones, Johnson, and Co. Bank.

" 'I met Winter some five years back,' said he. 'A man with a keen interest in our knowledge and a very sharp mind, he had the correct references and was, almost immediately, granted membership into our little group.' "

"A banking secretary. How very interesting. And is he currently employed in this trade?" I interrupted Watson's narrative.

"Simmons did not say," Watson replied. "I took his words to mean that he was still employed there, yes."

I winced at the presumption. "Nine days absent from his office would surely have excited some comment on the part of Winter's employers."

"I shall get to that, Holmes." Watson's reply was as peevish as one might expect. "In any event, I learned that Winter lived utterly alone in his modern heap of a suburban villa, and subsequently it was Simmons who found him. Winter's cousin they called in for politeness' sake, but it has been mainly Simmons and other high-ranking members of his order who have tended to him over this past week."

"In living alone and having a non-existent job at a bank, or one in which he has careless colleagues, how is it that Winter's condition was actually discovered?" I asked, exasperated.

"A very good question and one whose answer Simmons took great care to dodge," Watson said.

" 'We cannot know for certain how long Winter has remained in his unresponsive state. My estimate of nine days is just that: an estimate,' Simmons said. 'I found him locked in his bedroom —the key was still in the lock on the inside—and lying quietly upon the bed one week ago.'

"I still had in mind our working hypothesis, but I'll admit to a brief thrill when Simmons told me this," Watson interrupted his narrative once more. "An individual does not easily poison another and then orchestrate some method of locking the door to both house and inner room from the wrong side when they leave."

"I've at least a half a dozen cases where I can recall such creative acrobatics from a villain with regards to locked rooms," I drawled, eyes half-closed. "But continue."

Clearing his throat and shooting me another peevish glance, he said, "We entered a house wrapped in a heavy silence. The air of the rooms felt consecrated. Simmons and I were penetrating sacred secrets while remaining none the wiser for our transgression, suffering the fall of Adam without having tasted the apple. I could see this in the set of my companion's shoulders, his changed energy. A soul had gone a-wandering, and its echo flitted through the sunbeams which fell from the open windows.

"In contrast, Mr. Winter lay in darkness. Heavy curtains had been drawn, shrouding his room in uncertain gloom. The bed linens were drawn up tight under his chin, and he lay as a corpse awaiting burial. Still and still.

" 'If I may?' I asked and approached the bed.

" 'That is why you are here, is it not?' Simmons whispered back, not sullen, not resentful, not even hopeful, but merely factual.

"I grunted and consulted my black bag. After a brief examination of the patient, I replaced my stethoscope inside my hat and turned to Mr. Simmons. 'Your estimate is nine days?'

" 'Nine,' Simmons confirmed.

" 'Food? Drink?' I asked.

" 'He will take none.'

" 'Then I do believe he is merely sleeping. But it is a sleep of the most profound, most composed and complete sort as ever I have heard. Not a flicker of an eyelid or twitch of a muscle while I examined him,' I said.

" 'He will not wake, even under such encouragement as might call his soul back to him. Every spell. Every exhortation. We have tried every reasonable call to his senses.'

" 'Then you must try the unreasonable,' I replied.

" 'No!' Simmons' soft-spoken composure vanished. 'The danger to Winter if we— No, I will not leave him to languish as the others who went before but neither can I, in good conscience, threaten his life through our actions. But what can we do? What may we safely do for poor Mr. Winter?'

"Simmons paused, anguished indecision robbing him of easy answer.

" 'I must understand the nature of this danger if I am to attempt to rouse him. Nine days with neither food nor drink. Any longer and his death is almost assured,' I warned.

" 'Very well.' Simmons' eyes clung to Winter

as though the sleeping man were a life ring and he a castaway at sea. 'Members of our order, provided they have sufficient strength of will and personal commitment to the undertaking, are able to eject from their physical self their higher, intangible self. Winter has—to borrow the term—gone visiting. He has sent his vital essence elsewhere.'

" 'The soul.' I nodded.

" 'Not quite, but very near. For our purposes, however, the distinction is negligible and would unnecessarily complicate matters. Travelling astrally—that is, moving about our world and others via our astral selves—is nigh on limitless. Almost. The limit being, more or less, the connection to one's physical body left behind. We remain, while we yet draw breath, creatures who require a corporeal presence in the world, and this makes us vulnerable. Open to mischief. A traveller must therefore always take precautions.'

"I looked 'round me at the sombre room. 'A quiet, dedicated space removed from disturbances, for one.'

" 'Normally, a soul will come running back, quick as you like, when the body is disturbed. And so such travels, therefore, are best practiced in secret, in spaces where a person is unlikely to be interrupted. There are times—rare times—when the shock of a physical body recombining with its astral stuffs has caused . . . A sudden shock could well kill him. Though, at this point, doing nothing is, in itself, a death sentence, you are correct.'

" 'You say that three others have been afflicted in this manner?' I asked.

"Simmons replied, 'Winter is the third of our order to fall into such a state. The other two did not make it back to their physical selves.'

" 'The aforementioned shock?' I inquired.

"Simmons shook his head. 'They simply faded. Travelled away and never returned.'

" 'Could the fault be within the technique itself? Not some outside threat from an unseen enemy but some defect in how this visiting is attempted?' I asked.

" 'Anything is possible.' Simmons gave a wry smile. 'Which makes any such errors doubly my fault. I, myself, taught them the technique, you see. And I do not believe you were aware that I was practicing such magics when I came calling to 221B last night.'

"This last caught me, and I can see from your expression, Holmes, that it has you as well. I can return to that later for, at the time, Simmons' claims of responsibility had roused in me some of my own. I had a duty of care to a patient who threatened to simply fade away if actions were not undertaken. But then, any actions I took might have unforeseen and fearsome consequences. To sever a soul from a man's body . . . Did I believe Simmons' claims more than my own scientific knowledge? No. And so I undertook preparations for the type of interruption in which I had the most faith," Watson concluded.

I smiled. "Smelling salts?"

"Ha! Not in the least, Holmes," Watson chuckled. "Those had just then failed me on my initial examination. No response to light in the eyes or moving of the limbs. As Simmons said, Winter could not be coaxed to take food or drink. They had shouted and begged for nigh on a week and had nothing to show for it."

"Then what is it that you did, man?"

Watson smirked. "I lit Winter's room on fire."

It was my turn to laugh, and laugh I did. "You haven't any right, you know."

Warming to my reaction, Watson explained, "I built the punkiest fire that ever there was and sabotaged the flue. Lighting the mess, I entreated Simmons to join me in a lusty outcry, and on our third exclamation of 'Fire!' Winter practically leapt from his bed in alarm."

"And his soul, clearly, was still connected with his body?" I drawled, still chuckling as I lit my pipe.

"He was far too ill for me to besiege him with questions, but yes, Winter appeared to be perfectly unscathed from his ordeal. Simmons seemed both irate and infinitely grateful. We aired out the room and managed to get some broth into that weak and starving man," Watson said. "Triumphant and thinking this might well be the end of things unless further developments turned up, I took my leave. I was on the doorstep of Winter's house when a gentleman who had been loafing by the fence turned and made haste in the opposite direction. I ran him down, and pressed by my insistence, he introduced himself as a cohort to the man whose house I had just left. A Mr. King, by name."

LOCKED DOORS

CHAPTER 5

"'Tell me, has the worst happened?' said he.

"And I replied, 'Tell me who you are, sir, and why it is you lurk outside a man's home.'

"The man's eyes had settled upon my black bag, and he said, 'I am Mr. Frederick King, a friend of Mr. Winter's. Has he succumbed?'

"Now, your methods are fine and all, Holmes," Watson broke away from his tale, "but I will fully admit that I was momentarily at a loss as to how to proceed without compromising Simmons or Winter. I had a fear that I would disclose something which I ought not. I fell back upon my physician's training and said something or other about how Mr. King would have to apply to Mr. Winter himself for any sort of answer as I was not free to speak on such matters.

"I lifted my medical bag in illustration of my point and made as if to walk away.

" 'He lives, then!' King cried. Reaching out, he seized my hand and gave it a vigorous shake. 'Thank you, Doctor. He is alone in his house then? I may see him?'

"I had no choice but to accompany this Mr. King back to Winter's house." Watson shook his head. "Something in King's insistence, his remarkable enthusiasm, had grabbed hold of my imagination. Imagination, Holmes, yes, as I hadn't any one thing I could fixate on as the reason for my unease."

"His appearance?" I asked.

"Well-dressed and standing a little shorter than myself. Younger, too, by my estimate. I would have been surprised to learn if he had any occupation, and so, when I say he seemed a gentleman to me, I mean that in every way which my instincts could sense. What else? Kindly eyes and mouth. Pleasant manners—if one forgives his loitering outside of Winter's home. I would say that, overall, King is as present a person as Simmons is ethereal."

I frowned. So, Watson had gained the same indistinct impression of Simmons as I.

Watson continued on. "Mr. Simmons answered the door so quickly as to have me believing he had watched the entire exchange."

" 'Ah! Mr. King. So good of you to stop by,' Simmons said. 'Dr. Watson, Mr. King has been taking his turn at keeping a watch on Winter whilst he . . . slept.'

"He shut the door behind us, and freed from the prying eyes of the quiet street, he continued, 'King has only lately come amongst our sect. But he is a much-accomplished magician.'

"He turned to address King, surprising me with the following claim, 'Dr. Watson is a physician with an interest in our ideologies. With such a like-minded individual applying for inclusion into our brotherhood and with Winter's condition, I elected to have him help me with Brother Winter. He has performed most admirably.'

"King eyed me with new respect, and I do believe I passed inspection despite my shock over Simmons' unexpected words. He said, 'Winter?'

" 'He is sitting up in his room at this very moment.'

" 'May I see him?' King's palpable energies redirected themselves toward Simmons.

" 'Well, now.' Simmons appeared nonplussed and lowered his voice. 'Brother Winter has been through quite an ordeal. He may not be fully in capacity to handle questions.'

" 'Ah. Still, I cannot fault good news.' King smiled, then frowned. 'But not all the news is good.'

" 'What news? I had not heard anything,' Simmons said.

" 'The news I was bringing to you myself, so alarming and fresh as it was,' King intoned, lowering his voice though not so much that I could not hear.

"I considered. King had been standing outside of Winter's home. He had not asked over Simmons when I accosted him in the street. Was that in an effort to protect their order? Or had King's words just now been a lie?

"Mr. King thoughtfully thumbed the breast pocket of his coat. Mind made up, he sighed and brought out a slip of paper. A telegram. 'Received early this morning. From Mr. Davis. It would seem that someone gained access to our hall sometime in the night.'

"Simmons' eyes flashed. 'A burglary?'

" 'It would appear that the intruder had a key."

" 'But you believe them to be not counted amongst your membership?' I asked, in spite of myself.

"King did not seem to mind and turned to me saying, 'I would not have called it an incursion if they were one of our own, though it might be considered irregular. In that case, the fate of such a person would be for Simmons to decide. Regardless, Davis had previously confessed to me that the key entrusted to him had fallen out of his possession sometime late last week.'

" 'Lost?'

" 'Stolen?'

"Simmons and I spoke at once.

" 'Why is this the first I am hearing of this?' Simmons snapped.

"King glanced meaningfully into the upper reaches of Winter's house. 'You've been much occupied by other matters. I assumed the issue would clear itself up, that Mr. Davis would find the key having merely misplaced it.'

" 'King, if you would.' Simmons indicated the parlour with a jerk of his head, adding, 'Watson, would you see to Winter's comfort? We can come fetch you afterwards.'

"A little put off but more inclined to try my best to overhear what was about to be discussed than to catch a train home, I complied. There was opportunity in it which I was not about to waste.

"I had, in leaving Winter's house the first time, given my prescription on how best to bring him back to health. Simmons had written it down with the idea of forwarding my instructions to Winter's cousin, to whom he would send word of our patient's return to consciousness. Directing me to the kitchen so that I might administer this remedy myself led us to discover that Mr. Winter had no arrowroot on hand. Simmons offered to go to the shop down the lane.

"This had the benefit of giving me ample time for a strained but polite discussion with King. I was lucky that you were able to imbue me with some of your knowledge of Simmons' order and the others like it. The claim that I was interested in such a fellowship would have gone hard with me had I nothing of intelligence to say on the matter. I believe I came across exactly as I ought: inspired if wholly in the dark.

"King was more than willing to discuss small matters with me, his enthusiasm catching him up again in its grasp. I detected a disposition toward pride, too. He was, in theory, bound to silence per the rules of their order but seemed to me that he desperately wished to speak to any uninitiate who would listen.

"Simmons returned, and my having thrown together a healthful and easily digested decoction, I saw to Winter, leaving the two theosophists to their conversation in the parlour downstairs. The minutes ticked past while I fed some of the thick arrowroot gruel to the still frightfully weak Mr. Winter. His watery eyes followed my every movement.

"I caught him up on the events of the week, informing him that his colleagues Simmons and King were downstairs at that very moment, having sat by his bedside during his insensibility. Small talk of weather, the news, music filled the time and the silence between us.

" 'Thank you, Doctor,' Winter's paper-thin voice sounded at last, and I put aside the porridge. My patient's eyelids were drooping. While he had, of course, had more than enough sleep in the past few days, he was weak, he was fed, and he was comfortable. I let him slumber and moved to listen by the door.

"At intervals I could hear the occasional muttered syllable but nothing so clear as to discern what, exactly, the two men were saying. My hand was on the door handle, though what plan my brain was hatching, I knew not. I was not exactly going to sneak down the stairs and eavesdrop. Was I?

"Some strangeness, some odd feeling, gripped me. For a long moment, I stared unmoving at the door. And then I turned the handle. Or, rather, I tried to turn the handle. It resisted. The door was locked.

"I jerked back, nonplussed. Simmons and King had locked me in? As precaution against my spying upon their conversation or a mere oversight? Winter still slumbered peacefully at my back. As my patient's nerves were unlikely to stand much strain, hollering and banging on the door was out of the question.

"I chose to make the most of it and settled in to listen and watch and wait. But Simmons and King's discussion remained too quiet to make anything out. At length I heard them on the stairs. I backed away and was over by the window, fiddling with the curtains when they unlocked the door to set me free at long last.

"I wasted no time in voicing my annoyance over having found the door locked behind me. Neither seemed guilty in their response. Both appeared quite apologetic, in fact, each coming up with their own excuses and explanations for what must have happened. Some of these newer houses, you know. With the changing of the weather, a door can stick. Perhaps I was mistaken, and it had never truly been locked? Or . . . or, perhaps, there were powers at sway nearby. We had thwarted whoever had tried to do away with Winter. Mayhap that malevolence still hung about? King and Simmons made a big song and dance about checking the room, coming up uneasy but empty-handed.

"After that, I took my leave, Simmons and King thanking me profusely and each of us promising to be in touch in the coming days. I took the train back to Town, and here I am, none the worse for my strange morning's adventure." Watson ceased his narrative and waited for my reaction.

"Well then!" I sat back, surprised and intrigued. "You really ought to have used your time more productively while locked in Winter's sickroom, Watson. Listening at a keyhole for a conversation you might snatch five percent of is a waste of opportunity when a dastardly trick has been played on the occupant of the room and you've no idea how the man has been incapacitated. You concluded no poison from Winter's condition, true. But his condition was as bland as bland could be. Perhaps there was something, some clue, to be found within his sickroom to either satisfy or clear the suspicion of foul play."

Watson appeared aggrieved for my words.

I smiled warmly. "There is unexpected gain in today's events. I had planned on committing the cardinal sin of asking Simmons for a complete roll of his membership, but this does us one better and without the risk of a door being slammed shut in my face in the form of a firm 'no.' I recommend you join their Theosophical Order of Odic Forces, if they'll have you."

"Now see here—!"

"I cannot do this," I hurried to explain. "Whereas you've a rapport with them. It is up to you, Watson. My name is the name which immediately puts the ne'er-do-well on their guard. Yours inspires confidence. Your manner gains friendships and, if you'll pardon the expression, opens doors. You must write to Simmons and apply. Today. Tell him that the issue with the locked/not locked door has intrigued you all the further, and along with his words introducing you to King, you've gained a real interest, if they will have you. He is an intelligent man. He will know you intend to look further into his case under this guise. But it will give him the clear path he needs to allow you access to the order's innermost workings."

PLACED IN A DIFFICULTY

CHAPTER 6

Having agreed to my plan, Watson wrote to Simmons, who answered by calling upon us at Baker Street once more. This time he deigned to sit, though he declined any further offers of hospitality. I noted that he had a new hat.

He began with an apology. "I have certainly placed Dr. Watson in a difficulty. I had not anticipated Brother King's presence outside Winter's house and the questions it would, doubtlessly, spark. And with you not having accompanied Dr. Watson, Mr. Holmes, I found a ready excuse which King did not question. I suppose I will have to explain myself to him."

"Not at all, Mr. Simmons," Watson hurried to reassure him. "I would be glad to do what I may in the service of your case and find your order intellectually interesting, if far from what I might encounter in the course of my ordinary business. I can only hope that my having gone along with your claim does not put you in an awkward position with your members."

"Your feint has the potential to open up a line of investigation which we would be foolish to ignore. Watson is perfectly capable of acting in my stead in this matter," I drawled, not looking at Simmons. "He mentioned that there had been some sort of an incident at your order's sanctuary? Something about a key gone missing?"

"Why, yes, I had completely forgotten that Watson was present when King told me of the incident with Mr. Davis, one of our members. He misplaced his key—or assumed he had. Then, someone came into our hall one night last week, using, we presume, the missing key. They removed several items. Items ceremonial in nature. Most are easily replaced, candles and the like. A table was moved." Simmons' voice quivered slightly, and he trailed off.

"And you don't believe it was a member's doing?" I pressed.

"I do not know what to believe, save for these were not the actions of someone friendly to our faith." The quaver in Simmons' words grew stronger. "A table was moved. Small as it might seem to you, this is the act of an enemy. Things have their place. There is meaning and sacredness to how we array our hall. Petty burglary is one thing, but the reordering—not tossing about, but pointed replacement of items—is an insult to the space's sacred purpose."

"Thank you." I considered how at odds my own domestic habits were with that of Simmons and his order, suppressing a smile and a sigh of—what was this? Envy? "Presumably you've set things to rights?"

"Yes. I could not let time pass with things in that state." He shuddered.

"Ah, well, then there is little use in my profaning your order's inner sanctum with my presence," I said, moving on. "I still would, however, like to inquire into the circumstances surrounding the other two victims."

"At your leisure, Mr. Holmes, though only the one, Mr. William Henry, lived in Town. The other —" Simmons gulped and, for a moment, I had half a fear he would fall into a swoon. "For the other I would have to warn the family. It is a delicate situation, understand."

"The family did not know of the deceased's involvement in your order?" I asked.

"They did not, no. That would have been against our rules." Simmons shook his head. "In this instance, the greater difficulty lies in the fact that, at one time, Miss Eunice Overweg and I had been engaged to be married."

"This Miss Overweg, she was a formal member of the Theosophical Order?" Watson asked a little too sharply.

I sat forward in my chair, exchanging a quick,

chastising look with Watson. I agreed with his sentiment on behalf of Mrs. Jones' complaints, but there were times when my friend's sense of gallantry was downright inconvenient.

Simmons did not appear to notice and smiled ruefully as he answered, "A disciple, more accurately. And there is less impropriety or drama than I have led you to believe. Ours was a cordial separation. How could it not be, if she allowed me to remain in her life all this time? But her brother, he took affront to our changed affections and never forgave me."

"And this brother? He knew of your continued acquaintanceship with Miss Overweg?"

"Mr. Overweg and I were not on speaking terms, and I believe he was not particularly kind to his sister over her refusing to cut me from her life entirely. He is a good man, and I do not wish to cast him in a poor light, considering all that has happened," Simmons hurried to explain. "I will do what I can with regards to opening your path for a proper investigation, though with a scene months cold, I cannot say I have any hopes you will discover anything we or the police had not."

I had lost myself to pondering, reordering the facts in my mind and reconfiguring what I already knew so as to produce new threads of thought. I seized one and followed it, asking, "This astral travel, which appears so dangerous yet so indistinct—if you'll forgive me—how exactly is it accomplished? Watson reported to me that, in his professional medical opinion, Winter was merely suffering from acute malnutrition."

"Yes," Watson spoke up. "Might we have, from you, more information on how the process works? Again, if astral travel is the method by which your enemy attacks, it would be helpful to know its rules and its methodology. How this activity, for example, lends itself to causing the type of weakness I observed in Winter and which you say came from his sending his vital self elsewhere."

"Remember that the good doctor here has a keen and proper interest in becoming a novitiate in your order," I offered. "I would be content in understanding whether or not fellow householders might know of the activities of your constituents, were said activities taking place within their own homes. Membership in your order and the promise of silence on that point, granted, a person locking themselves into a bedroom or study for hours on end and—well, what is it they do? Are there preparations to be made? Specific attire? Words to be said? I have some experience with meditation practices from my travels abroad these past three years. Mesmerism, too. The mind is a powerful vehicle."

"Winter has fully embraced suburban bachelor life and so lives utterly alone. He remains the sole witness to his ordeal, and he has claimed no memory of events save for fragmented dreams," Simmons said. "Mr. Henry was a father of three. Married. I do not believe anyone in his household considered themselves to be lying to the police with their statements of fact, per se. A man's business is his own, particularly when foul play is not suspected."

"Suspected by the authorities," I added, smiling grimly.

"I did not ask questions. At the time, I thought as the police did: a tragic, unexpected passing. Something to do with the heart." Simmons shuddered. "As for Miss Overweg, she had her brother —who was guardian in name and reputation alone. His business keeps him away more than he is present. His household supports some staff. In her case, I do not believe anyone much questioned her activities, hers being a free spirit under a freer hand.

"But to your question, Mr. Holmes, Mr. Watson, the sending of a double is as simple—and as difficult—as any magic I can manage."

"And the dangers?"

Simmons smiled. "The body—the physical body—loves its astral self and will not part easily with it. Certainly one should take precautions to prevent disturbance, for it is this which poses the greatest threat. The silver cord which binds the astral self to the body is as strong as any matter on earth. It is malleable and near-infinitely stretched. Thus, it takes an act of concentrated evil to separate the two, but yes, that is the danger we have all been facing of late.

"The travelling itself is as safe as the will of the

magician is strong. Simplicity itself, though beyond the reach of most anyone save those who have made a particular study of it. Concentration without concentration and requiring no special circumstances save for the aforementioned privacy. If a person wishes to be comfortable during their undertaking, I recommend it. The moon phase ought to be consulted. Or it may be disregarded altogether. A quiet space, a dedicated amount of time of any duration, and a qualified magician may simply will their non-physical essence into separation. I, myself, use the receiving room on the first storey of my house. I find it comfortable, amply situated, and, as I live alone and keep set hours, free from disturbance. From there I have visited the far-flung reaches of our Earth. I have looked into the doings of the artists who paint along the Rhine. I have seen cathedrals and castles and other worlds beyond our own which defy description."

Watson shifted in his seat, and Simmons glanced to him, certain he had lost his audience. With a sigh, our guest rose and went to collect hat and coat. "Gentlemen, I will be in touch; Watson, I will be seeing you."

At the door he turned. "Oh, and perhaps you would be interested to know that on my first visit here, it was only my astral double which you met."

Mr. Simmons left two dumbfounded men in his wake. Watson was appalled, I merely bemused.

"Now you see what you have gotten me into,

Holmes," my friend grumbled, settling into a chair and taking up his pipe.

"I see, yes." I sat and struck a match to my own briarwood. "Besides the secrecy to which they all swear and the strange looks they might solicit from the likes of Gregson and company were they to be forthright in their order's beliefs and activities, the complex circumstances of Simmons' relationship to Miss Overweg is certainly another reason for Simmons to have been reluctant in the idea of appealing to the police rather than ourselves."

"Miss Overweg." Watson frowned. "Considering that Mrs. Jones said that women are not allowed in Simmons' order and her own past with the man, you do not suppose . . . ?"

"That there are more connexions betwixt these cases than initially thought?" I completed his question. "No. I would not venture into the realm of fancy quite so energetically. We've other journeys of the mind to undergo."

"Beg pardon?"

I ignored Watson's cautioning glance, and our conversation died to heavy silence.

"There is, too, the attractiveness of the powers which Simmons claims to command. In the right young lady, it could sound romantic ideals," Watson added at length.

"Perhaps Miss Overweg, and others, reading 'romance' where there is merely 'religion'? It is possible. I think it likely, actually, considering there are now at least two women from Simmons' past who are involved in his men-only order to some degree. How many others?"

It was unfair of me to use Watson's chivalry against him. But in turning his mind to imaginary, ill-used damsels in distress, I diverted the energies that he would otherwise have wasted on me and the line of questioning which I could feel developing.

Thus, we smoked in companionable quietude, the thick, aromatic smoke carrying our remaining unspoken ideas from our lips and into the realm of tangible visibility. They swirled about the centre of the room, perhaps knocking themselves into invisible lurking auras, spirits in search of rest, weary wanderers looking for answers.

HOW VS WHY

CHAPTER 7

"I thank you, Mr. Turner, for your swift response to my message. And I thank you for agreeing to meet here, at Baker Street, so that we might speak candidly," I said, gesturing that my visitor have a seat.

Mr. Daniel Turner gave one thoughtful turn in place before adopting a spot in the middle of 221B's couch. I had the distinct impression that he was measuring the room, though with what mental ruler I could not begin to fathom. Tidy and trim, with a shock of white hair and sweeping moustaches to match, the head magician for the Society of Universal Energies was here at my invitation. An appointment I had pointedly made with the knowledge that Watson would be out for the morning.

"And I thank you for your interest, Mr. Holmes, in our little club." Mr. Turner gave a wry smile.

"Come, Mr. Turner, you may be frank with me in this matter, considering my interest."

"Your interest," he mused over my words. "Forgive me, Mr. Holmes, but when a man of your intellectual prowess—and, granted, we have many a genius amongst our numbers—when someone such as yourself approaches, I can only surmise that you are doing so from a place of profane scepticism or from one of deep conviction, blessed with the spirit of divine inquiry."

"Can it not be both, when a person knows as little as myself?"

Satisfied by my answer, Mr. Turner's smile turned warm. He asked, "And what is it you wish to know?"

Under his piercing gaze, a shudder passed through me as though lightning had discharged close by. I felt exposed by the direct question. I felt the echo of that horrible, desperate excitement which I had experienced the evening of my first becoming acquainted with Mr. Percy Simmons. And I feared disinvitation, removal from a company of faith whose acceptance I had yet to gain. What was it I wished to know, Mr. Turner? I wished to know to what end any of us are alive.

But my needs were too fearsome to put into words, and so I said, "I can tell at a glance where a man has walked from the dirt upon his shoes, discern marital bliss—or a lack thereof—from the state of a hat or watch chain. Carpets and door latches whisper their stories in stray hairs and scuff marks. The heart of a mystery opens itself to me like a flower, whereas for others such answers remain shrouded in the gloom of a wintertime freeze. I understand what motivates a person to act—most generally when the motives are for ill. I can see all the pieces in the puzzle, Mr. Turner. I see how they fit, what picture they will make. But what I don't know is: why the picture?"

Mr. Turner remained silent for several long moments as he considered my words. Had he spoken without any hesitation, I would have been disappointed. Had he tried to answer in the here and now, I would have known my question disregarded or, worse, misunderstood. Instead, my guest rose, tugged his sleeves, sniffed, measured the room with his eyes again, and said, "We will be in touch, Mr. Holmes."

I saw my visitor out, and now strangely ill-at-ease over having had to admit, out loud, something over which I felt true disquiet, I paced the carpet and mentally catalogued where I stood on my various tasks for the week. It did not take long. A mountain of reading awaited me. Various correspondence, books, pamphlets, and newspapers sat neglected upon my desk.

Throwing myself at the disparate collection, I gave myself over to the solving of nearly a dozen cases which had been entrusted to me. Bountiful brainwork, it held my attention for some minutes.

At length I sat back, glared at the rest of the tasks at hand, and then cast equal annoyance at the clock for good measure. No amount of willing time to pass would move the sunbeams which slanted across my path.

I reached for my violin.

I was still playing when, sometime later, I discovered that Watson had returned home and now sat quietly at our dining table. He had a curious charmed look about him, and self-conscious, I put down my bow.

"My apologies, Watson, I had not heard you come in," I explained.

"By all means, Holmes, do keep playing," he said. "I do not believe I've heard anyone—much less you—play like that in all my days."

I noted that the lighting within our apartment had changed. A glance to my watch confirmed it; for all my frustrations and efforts, in the end the morning had gone in the blink of an eye.

"Your extemporaneous little compositions are usually so morose," Watson continued. "Whatever mood sparked today's playing is a thing to be encouraged. Unmusical to the point of distraction, certainly, but . . . beautiful."

I frowned as, with Watson's observation, my mind's eye conjured up the image of Turner sitting upon our couch. For I had felt something of the ethereal while I had scraped mindlessly at my instrument. It was as though something had passed through Baker Street. Some scent, some cleansing breeze. It was introspection approaching the exquisite, a thing with which I had little experience. Freed from this terrestrial plodding, I had soared. And now I was back earthbound, trudging amongst the clay. I placed my violin back in its corner, distancing myself from the sublime which I had unintentionally touched and which I might never again reach, save through the accident of a distracted mind.

"Come, I'll ring for lunch," I offered, pulling at the bell. "And here is a note from Mr. Simmons."

I handed over the short letter to Watson who read it aloud:

"Mr. Holmes and Mr. Watson,

"I made my appeal to the family of Mr. Henry and discovered that they have gone abroad for their period of mourning. The house is let, and so, save for if you wish to look into what the police concluded in their brief examination of the scene from last January, I have no answer save to beg your patience.

"I have been equally put off in my inquiries into the affairs of the late Miss Overweg. Her brother has yet to respond to my appeals. Thus, I must ask that you wait until I can manage these various circumstances.

"With apologies and thanks for your continued patience,

"Yours, etc. etc., Simmons."

Watson looked to me over the top of the page

in his hand, exasperation lining his features. "It would be far easier on me, Holmes, if I did not have to read correspondence from the man and think of our acquaintance with him in one way and have to treat with him publicly in another."

"Ah." I rubbed my hands together. "Details, details, Watson."

"Well, for one thing, I called upon Mr. Winter, and I agree with Simmons' assessment. The man appears to know even less than we of his ordeal."

"And medically?"

"Medically, he's on the path to recovery and shows no signs of any ill treatment. I fully believe he put himself into that state with his nerves. He seems a careless, dreamy sort of man. I suspect he neglected himself until he was too far gone to be roused by anything save for that emergency which I concocted upon our first meeting."

"Thank you, Watson." I gestured he proceed.

Watson paused, indecisive, then said, "King was interested in my travels in the service—"

I pursed my lips.

He tried again. "Simmons is contemplating replacing Mr. Davis, per his . . . What is it, Holmes?"

I waved a hand. "This is gossip. I need fact. I need what they do and where they do it and why they do it."

"Whatever does it matter?" Watson was nonplussed.

"Because that is the case as stated to us by

Simmons. Right or wrong, that is the angle we must take unless something more concretely criminal comes along. I am even less satisfied than yourself, Watson." I had softened my tone and aimed for the safety of commiseration. Rescue was at hand in the opening of the door, and I turned my attentions there. "Ah, Mrs. Hudson, thank you; we are both of us famished."

Our landlady bustled about setting up our table and tut-tutting. "This is for one of your little problems, no doubt. Well, when you change your mind, do let me know. I can produce this as easily as the usual."

"Thank you, Mrs. Hudson, for your invaluable contributions to justice in England," I purred and saw her out. It being midday, Watson did not at first discover that his brandy and my whisky were both no longer in attendance on the sideboard. His dismay at the contents of the day's fare, however, was a dissatisfaction soon voiced.

"This is your doing, is it not?" Watson's narrow-eyed accusation came with the smallest of smiles.

I had upon my plate potato rolls, a generous helping of vegetable pie, and some sort of bread stuffing. I gestured that he follow suit, saying, "I have requested that Mrs. Hudson provide us with a less indulgent cuisine while we await your induction into the Theosophical Order of Odic Forces, per their tenets."

"You mean the ascetic life. Which, in this

instance, appears to consist of an abstinence from meat and alcohol," Watson observed. "I do believe I had more than my share of the Spartan lifestyle while in the service, but if you deem it necessary, Holmes, I will do what I must."

"We, Watson. We will," I said.

SOUL-SEARCHING

CHAPTER 8

"**I** came straight here." Mrs. Jones sat in the cane chair by 221B's hearth, trembling.

Watson was, again, out for the moment, and unlike during my clandestine meeting with Mr. Turner the week before, today I dearly missed the doctor's presence. For our client's nerves seemed stretched to breaking. With as poorly as she appeared to me, it was a wonder Mrs. Jones had made it to my doorstep without mishap.

In my hands: a new incriminating diary page —complete with envelope this time, though it had become tearstained in Mrs. Jones' distress. The suggestions from the previous portion of the entry had now been fulfilled in the form of the narrator's declaring ardent affection for the man to whom she was not married. While less carnal than that which had been sent to Mrs. Jones weeks before, the contents were so emotionally charged as to provide a new angle of danger to my client's reputation. From her blushing and stammering, and the aforementioned trembling, I could see that Mrs. Jones' statement about her improper relationship with Mr. Simmons was neither as short-lived nor as trivial as she had initially claimed.

It was this issue that I addressed first, asking, "In your estimate, how long is a moment of weakness, Mrs. Jones?"

Cooing and consolation might have tipped my client over into hysterics, whereas my uncompassionate question had a sobering effect. The quivering frailty ceased, and goaded into anger—and frank honesty—Mrs. Jones found strength. She eyed me coldly. "An individual may love more than one person at a time. My affair with Simmons was as short-lived as I have previously claimed, Mr. Holmes, while it was the state of my resisting having a heart divided which had any duration at all."

"Would that you could show this fire and harbour such convictions for yourself when you next anticipate the mail, madam," I said. "You are a widow now and thus have no husband to injure with these split affections. True, your actions from ten years past are indelible, but as you yourself have told me, said actions are unlikely to hamper any monies you might have received on your husband's passing. This secret holds less danger to you than what injury you give yourself in your anxiety."

"But it is a secret! It is my secret! Mine and Mr. Simmons'," cried Mrs. Jones. "It is a secret which I wish to remain hidden from the world. And it is my hope that you may put a stop to whomever is tormenting me with these letters."

She rose and began to pace the room. "I fear I shall go mad. Perhaps I already am. Perhaps I did write these . . . these . . . pages. But how could I not remember? In what state must I have been to have only fear in the place of memory?"

And how is it that someone else has the pages in hand, unbeknownst to Mrs. Jones, I wondered. I said, "I have been asking my questions and looking into the activities of three of the most capable forgers known to me. The exactitude of both the visual match and writing tone of the pages from your blackmailer when compared to writings authenticated by yourself are astounding, to say the least."

Again, questions of "why" and "how" continued to haunt me, questions I did not wish to force anew upon my client. For if blackmail was the aim, how could there not be a price exacted from Mrs. Jones? And with no price exacted from Mrs. Jones, how was it the mystery correspondent paid their skilled forger? If, indeed, these pages were forgeries.

With Mrs. Jones' latest arrival, the evidence in hand had doubled. Now was the time for my assurances, and I rose to my feet, saying, "I will be in touch, Mrs. Jones, and you can be certain that I will do my very best to get to the bottom of this matter, whatever the motive."

She thanked me and left.

Both diary pages and the lone envelope accompanied me to the desk. Under strong lamp light and a powerful lens, the stationery gave up little to my eyes. It was as it had been from the first. The writing style was a fine, if not a perfectly exact, emulation of that which Mrs. Jones had given to me for comparison, right down to how the pen performed under the pressure of the author's fingers. The stationery of this new page, the same as the old. Nothing appeared newer, falser, or stranger than before. The envelope: a cheap, commonplace little thing which anyone might have on hand. The writing on the envelope, however . . . this engrossed me for a good long while.

In the end, I was reasonably certain that it was a right-handed individual, possibly a man with fairly short fingers and shorter patience. They certainly held the pen in a curious fashion. Educated, per the quality and consistency of the penmanship. And the speed at which the address had been put upon the page told me that the writer was either not interested in hiding their hand or skilled at having more than one form of longhand easily available to them.

"That is either a point in favour of one of my forgers or a point against the whole of this case, in that the writer has little fear that Mrs. Jones will recognise them by their hand," I muttered. I was still engaged in pointless examination of the papers, making no further progress but having little else to go on, when Watson returned to Baker Street.

"Good afternoon, Holmes," he cried, taking up a glass and cigar before settling heavily onto our couch.

"Good afternoon." I glanced at the clock, surprised to note that it was, indeed some time after noon. "Shall I ring Mrs. Hudson for some lunch?"

He waved the words away with a groan. "For you, perhaps. But I've just come from that vegetarian restaurant over on Water Lane where I dined with Simmons and King."

I turned more fully from my papers and lens to eye my friend. "No initiation?"

"No." Watson's frustrations made the word sharp. "Nothing but lunch and conversation. Both entirely without meat. Again. By the by, I thank you for having regulated my diet so that Messrs. King and Simmons did not have to. Regardless, I've a fear they'll get more from me in the end than I from them. They say they want me for the Order, but then—"

"It's a case, Watson," I warned, sensing keen disappointment in addition to everything else.

"It's a case, yes. Your case." He cast a glare my way. "But I am the one who has to sit and blather on with them about the nature of the soul and the grand opportunities afforded a man who can harness ancient powers. They want to change the world. Two small men who think they alone have knowledge of the fabric of the universe."

"Don't they?"

My phlegmatic question was met with bland annoyance from Watson.

I repeated the question, "Don't they, though? In the past six months, three lives within their tiny order have been either deeply disturbed or utterly destroyed by these powers. Call it magic, call it mind; something in their keeping has touched, pretty deeply, the fabric of our universe."

"To that end," Watson began. "King managed to secure me all to himself for a moment post-luncheon. Simmons had business in Town, and rather than going his separate way from me, Mr. King thought it prudent to share a cab with me to my destination."

"Talking secrets."

"Talking secrets, yes." Watson nodded. "He asked me if Simmons had told me the full story regarding Winter's situation with regards to the Order. I told him that I had been informed that Winter was the third to lose his astral self while unconscious."

" 'Ah, but that is where you are wrong,' he said. 'Winter was the third of Simmons' theosophists to be endangered. One, the first by the name of Henry, did die in just that way. His family reported his death, and our understanding

of the circumstances had us concluding that he had sent his inner self away and not come home. But the second . . .'

"Here King leaned close, and once more, I felt his awesome magnetism grip me. He said, 'The second—a Miss Overweg—died by suicide.' "

" 'Suicide!' I said. 'Are you certain?'

" 'Without a doubt. She left a note.'

" 'How tragic. But how is it that Miss Overweg was a member of your order?'

"King smiled. 'She was not. But Simmons? He is our leader and does as he pleases. You can see all the more why he was reticent to provide you the full details. Perhaps that puts you off your interest in our order?'

" 'Not in the least,' I said. 'Though I would like to know why a suicide was considered by Simmons to be an attack from an enemy magician. Surely Miss Overweg's actions were her own. What did the police have to say about it?'

" 'The right observation, Dr. Watson. The right observation,' King said, his voice warming with encouragement. 'The police did not have the full facts. We know that Miss Overweg was travelling astrally right before her death, for her journey was made under Simmons' direct supervision. She wanted to see the worlds beyond, and he would make it so that she could. Ill-advised. Ill-conceived. The travelling went wrong. Just as with the others but different. Miss Overweg thrashed about on her bed. Simmons witnessed the battle for her physical body, and when Miss Overweg came to, she was not herself. Two days later she died, having ingested rat poison.'

" 'Oh my!' I said.

"King nodded sagely. 'Add to that Winter's misadventures and Simmons' feuding with no less than two other theosophic groups over his position on whether or not women ought to be included amongst our ranks, and I fear that it may not be to your benefit to press for your initiation. I tell you this because I care and because I worry that Simmons has only told you what benefits him to say.'

" 'What benefits him to say . . .' I mused, thoughtful.

" 'I have my knowledge and skill to protect me, Watson,' King said gently. 'As a new initiate, you would have all of the access but none of the power. You aided Winter, yes. But if Winter was a mistake of Simmons' . . . Now I have said too much and fallen into the trap of accusation. Heresy. I want you in our order. I do. To my mind, Simmons is too slow, too choosy in his recognition of aptitude.'

" 'Do you truly feel there is danger to me if I pursue my membership in the Odic Forces?' I asked.

" 'There is danger everywhere in this world, Doctor. But when we decide to enter other worlds as well?' King smiled. 'I apologize. I have done my friend a disservice in voicing my fears. We have suffered a great run of misfortune. Many would call that an encounter with evil itself and my accusation inspired by that same evil.'

" 'And do you, King, believe in evil? Personally?' I asked.

"His smile widened. 'But of course. Else I would have no faith whatsoever. Does not goodness require a devil for the satisfaction of its own definition?'

"And with that, I had arrived at my destination. Not here," Watson hastened to add. "I am not so much a fool as to lead King to Baker Street and compromise Simmons' case. Regardless, with King's words I now have concerns over Simmons and his motives in all of this. His connection with Jones. The timing of everything and the fact that he is quick to cry foul but take very little action himself."

I shifted in my chair, annoyed. "Simmons may express his fears and concerns, and King may do the same, and you pick one side over the other, Watson?"

"King is . . ." Watson struggled to find the words. "He is courteous and cool. He inspires. Simmons, he provokes. He provoked Mrs. Jones into being unfaithful—"

"Her actions are her own," I snapped. "Do not discount her agency within her own life."

Watson appeared taken aback. "I am sorry, Holmes. I am. But as someone who, beg pardon, has actually loved, has actually made the commitment of marriage to another, I do have to question Mrs. Jones on a fundamental level."

With that our conversation was over. I grabbed my coat, thanked Watson tersely for his report, and embarked upon one of my long rambles about the city.

Good. Evil. Justice. Faith. We could now add "love" to the list of broad and critical, soul-seizing concepts which I, apparently, could not grasp.

DOUBLES AND PAIRS

CHAPTER 9

I had managed alone in Baker Street in the three years leading up to the events in Switzerland. Led away by love, Watson had married our former client, Miss Mary Morstan. I did not begrudge him his happiness, though I did mourn, in my own way, his absence. I had learned of her untimely passing at a period when I was unable to return and be of use to my friend, and thus I had mourned anew but for different reasons.

The black band had gone from his hat by the time of my coming home to London. In Watson's eagerness for change, to rejoin me in my adventures, I neglected to consider the still-raw state of his heart. I could not understand, yes, but Watson was wrong. I loved.

Or, he was right. How might a person like me love? Me, who recoiled from feeling, from thinking about feeling, as though it were poison. Who could stand afar and coldly, impassively, watch John conclude that my death had occurred and do nothing.

My walk began while I was terribly, hotly angry. Angry over Watson's unbending, judgmental righteousness. Angry with myself for past actions and inactions. Angry for wanting to flee rather than feel. Angry for feeling in spite of fleeing. At length my walk transitioned into work as I abandoned my planned circuit for a path far more useful. My mind required engagement lest I find myself standing outside of the hall for the Theosophic Order of Odic Forces or worse, a church. The likes of Mr. Simmons and Mrs. Jones might be doing their level best to spirit their way into my senses at all hours, but I had other cases on my docket.

A quick bit of observation at the top of Haymarket in service to a smuggling case occupied my attentions, if little of my brains. I amused myself by contemplating the transcendence of the self, imagining that the smoke which billowed out of my mouth and curled up thinly from the end of my cigarette was my astral Other. With a cynical exhalation, I sent my misty double out into the skies to learn what he might.

In the end, I learned nothing while accumulating my tidy pile of ash. Irked, I dug about in my pockets and found that I had one card upon me. This I left for Mr. Turner some six streets over. I still had hopes of producing some definite results through membership in, or at least ready acquaintance with, the Society of Universal Energies. I might banter with Watson on the topic of locked room mysteries, but I truly disliked a case in which every door was barred and closed to me. A challenge was one thing. A pointed exclusion from all useful information quite another. I had leads, were I allowed to follow them. Mr. Frederick King, for example, had proved to be one of the rare individuals to evade my series of indexes. He was as hid from the public eye as was the very organization and beliefs he professed. In my pursuit of Turner's Society, I was going off a footnote of a footnote of a footnote.

I could only hope that my own induction into their hallowed ranks might pace alongside Watson's inclusion to Simmons' brethren of the Odic Forces. Two half-truths could make for a whole one, could they not?

Half-truths. Partial truths. Invisible, obvious, naked, made-up claims, facts, and fancies. I both hated and delighted in this case. It was veiled. It was as far from ordinary as I had managed in a long, long while. Normalcy vexed me. Safety repelled. I had hit my pinnacle and returned home triumphant and at long last to . . . To what, exactly? I was playing a game over and again when, truly, all I wanted to do some days was flip the board and be done with it.

"What is it you want, Sherlock?" I breathed fire with my question, leaning on the building opposite that of the leader of the Society of Universal Energies and burning the last of my cigarettes between my fingers. Impassive, I watched the embers creep ever closer to my thumbnail, waiting for the burn, the reminder that I was alive.

Positive proof. Scientific methodology. I needed to test the system, to test good and evil and justice. And to desperately hope that it wouldn't break under the strain. I needed Simmons to be wrong in his beliefs. I needed him to be right. I needed to be pushed to the edge, to dangle there, and this time have the leisure to see where it was I stood before choosing to live or to fall.

The door to Mr. Turner's house opened, and I shrank back into the long shadows of the coming evening. Fool, why? You have every right to linger here, to think and ponder and be. But the individual who hurried out was a servant intent on some secret errand.

Disgusted with myself, I turned westward and let instinct, traitorous though it may be, guide my steps until I found myself at the doorway of a local boxing club. My membership therein was on an on-again off-again nature. Frankly, I was too inconstant to pay proper dues and two of the men within too grateful from past services rendered to ever demand adherence on my part. I entered and was welcomed.

I spent the better part of fifteen minutes burning through the more hateful of my energies.

It was as anti-case an action as I could find in that hour in that quarter of the City, and it left me tired, if still unsatisfied in soul.

At last my patience and skills were spent, and as a reward for my efforts, I had to step from the ring with a split lip and dizzied senses. A familiar face, one from three and a half years past, came to stand by my side.

"Shaw." With a nod, I acknowledged him.

"So it is true that you've returned from the dead," he said. "And from the state of your lip, you bleed like the rest of us mortals. Come, have a beer with me."

"No, thank you, I've sampled the claret," I quipped. I eyed the old boxer. "You've not stayed untouched yourself. You're guarding one side instinctively. Left knee? You ought to let it heal before it leads to someone taking advantage."

He ignored my advice. "That fellow there, the one who led you to stand over here by me, he's quite the opponent, yes? Your abilities have not diminished since I last saw you, else you could not have stood long against such a fighter. And yet . . ." He paused to reflect. "And yet I do worry. You've a new intensity about you, Mr. Holmes, if you'll forgive my saying so. You have never been either merciless or cruel when you fight, but you fight with such precision, such calculated coldness. It adds a layer which, in a lesser man than you, could be dangerous. Even in a venue such as this. You fight like a man playing chess, as if your fists are bishops and your feet rooks—"

"And my head my queen," I finished.

"No," Shaw corrected. "Your head a pawn."

I looked sharply at my companion, surprised at the insight.

Seeing my look, he continued, "You fight as if it were matter of life and death and yet also as if you dearly wish to lose."

"These are testing grounds," I countered, looking back to where two men grunted and shuffled about in the ring. "A fellow can afford such experiments here."

"Mr. Holmes!" The club's instructor, a Mr. Brown, approached. "Whoever are you talking to, and however did you split your lip? I hadn't seen you step into the ring."

"Hello, Mr. Brown." I offered out my hand. "Shaw and I were just discussing—"

"Who?" Brown appeared puzzled.

"Mr. Shaw, a member as old and inconstant in attendance as myself," I laughed and turned and found I stood alone, save for Mr. Brown, of course.

Brown looked at me strangely. "Mr. Shaw has not come 'round these parts for a longer time than even yourself, Mr. Holmes. That's eighteen months since his knee failed him in the ring, and rather than risk the type of injury that leads a man to a worser way of life, he gave up boxing."

"I must have been mistaken," I replied, more

disturbed than I would let on. "That is what I deserve for letting myself get tapped and for being absent more often than I am present."

Brown laughed. "He must've tapped you good, the man who coloured your lip. Glad to see you're still in good form, Mr. Holmes. Oh, and I've a cousin who has been dealing with some little issue, if I might be so bold as to mention your name to them?"

"Send your cousin my way, yes," I said, extricating myself from the discomfiting conversation by way of noting the time and making some excuse or other about having somewhere I needed to be.

Out in the slanted sunlight and softened shadows of early evening, my aborted walk-into-work from earlier became truly aimless at last. I did not think on my non-encounter with Mr. Shaw. I could not and so I did not. Eventually I turned myself homeward and returned to 221 to find Watson in the process of donning coat and hat.

"Ah! I won't have to leave a message with Mrs. Hudson, then," he greeted me, handing over a telegram. "Holmes, I—"

Watson bit off his words and waited while my eyes scanned the paper in my hand.

PRESENCE REQUESTED AT ONCE. NEW DEVELOPMENTS. 26 HILL. SIMMONS.

. . .

"Addressed to you," I mused.

"She must mean for us both to come," Watson said. He knew better than to venture guesswork.

I held the door, and off we went.

Watson whistled the cab and, upon embarking, finally turned to me to complete his apologies. "What I said earlier was thoughtless. Both to you and to our client."

"You, Watson, live under the mistake of believing everyone to hold to the same values as yourself," I said. "At times it is a noble sentiment, particularly in my line of work where I rarely see or expect to see the best in a person. But, yes, today your mores did you little credit."

I paused, settling my gaze ahead before continuing, "Then again, something reliable, something constant, would be a consolation. Of all the topics which I have undertaken the task of becoming a temporary expert, this one is proving the most vexing. Different methods. Contradictory beliefs and practices. Yeats is—"

"The poet?"

"The very same. He is one of Them, you know. His poetry is proving most instructive, would you believe. Poetry. Ha!" I laughed, coldly. "The more I think on it, the more I try to fix a fact upon its face, the more push-back I receive. The veil. The veil resists my probing mind. There are, I believe, truths we are not meant to know. The universe protects herself from the minds of men. Perhaps . . . perhaps that truly is where evil has its origin."

"Evil, I believe, stems from a mind which refuses to make inquiry."

"Quite so." I flashed a quick smile. "Quite so, Watson. But it is frustrating all the same."

"Well, from what I understand of it from Simmons' and King's discussions with me, their order is attempting to resolve the beliefs of any number of religions from any number of cultures. Things not meant to go together. The pattern must be dizzying."

"And the brain subsequently rebels," I said. "Many paths up the same mountain, and an individual cannot walk them all at once. The premise is an interesting one, nonetheless. The idea that, underneath each seemingly contradictory truth, there lies a power which man may assert for the good of all."

"Or the ill."

"Or the ill," I agreed, thinking again of our client and wondering what new development awaited us at the end of our short journey back to Hill Street.

MY COLLEAGUE, MR. HOLMES

CHAPTER 10

We rang at Number 26 and were admitted by Judy, the maid who had been out last we were at Mrs. Jones'. A quiet, aggravated-looking young woman, she showed us into the next room where two gentlemen waited. Mr. Simmons I already knew. And, per Watson's previous descriptor, I presumed the other to be Mr. King. I was glad to note that, without my hardly having had to glance his way, Watson had mastered his own bewilderment.

"Dr. Watson. You received our telegram." Simmons strode forward with his hand outstretched. "I thank you for your haste. Your patient, the lady of the house, Mrs. Jones, is upstairs. She is conscious, but something has shaken her nerves, and she—well, you'll see soon enough."

"You'll have heard of my partner, Mr. Holmes?" Watson made the introductions, a hasty cover for the surprise of my presence. "Mr. King. Mr. Simmons. Two gentlemen who I have the pleasure of serving in a medical capacity of late."

"As well as social, Doctor." King smiled warmly, turning to grasp my hand in his. He said, "I was the one who insisted on Mrs. Jones having a doctor. What with Watson here having some familiarity with a recent misfortune of a similar nature, he was the logical choice. I hadn't any idea, through our brief acquaintance, that he was a colleague to the celebrated Mr. Sherlock Holmes."

"My apologies for my coming upon you gentlemen unexpectedly," I offered. "Just as Dr. Watson here has become accustomed to accompanying me upon my little cases, I too have sometimes assisted him when the need arises."

"Not at all, not at all." King smiled broadly. "You have some familiarity with the Winter case then, Mr. Holmes?"

I shook my head. "Only so much as to know that the unfortunate gentleman was meant to have spirited himself off somewhere—after a fashion—leaving his body behind to take ill. Watson said that he roused quickly enough under the proper stimulation. That along with the cryptic nature of today's telegram had me believing I might become of use."

"Cryptic," King repeated, for the first time looking morose. "I had not thought my words would come off as mysterious. Not so much so as to gain the attentions of Sherlock Holmes himself.

Again, granting that I hadn't made the connection with our Watson from the first. Simmons, you had the address. Were you aware with whom our neophyte shared celebrated acquaintance?"

Thunderstruck, Simmons smiled his disclaimer.

I too smiled, ready to play King's game, now that I had a better grasp on things. "The allusion to 'new developments' set alongside an address Watson has no prior familiarity with is suggestive, at the very least—potentially sinister when coupled with Simmons' name and the nature of the previous complaint which Watson saw to. At this hour, I would expect drawn curtains and, instead, find that I may see all the way into the airy darkness of a household much disturbed and a cab drawn up outside. Menace enough for you, sir, for me to decide upon entry rather than a farewell to my friend and continuing on of my own errands for the evening?"

Simmons called out over his shoulder. "Next he'll be telling you all about yourself, King. Watch yourself."

"Could you?" King's eyes lit up. "I have heard a number of accounts on how you're able to guess at all a man has done or might do."

I sniffed. "Let us see to your Mrs. Jones first."

Watson remained silent during the brief exchange, and I could feel his discomfort as he trailed us up the stairs. I could practically feel his eyes upon our backs, the rehearsed apologies he was planning for Baker Street—Bah! I had made the same error!—and the careful commitment to saying as little as he could in the here and now.

"We informed Mrs. Jones of your coming, Dr. Watson," King turned to address my friend. "For all that it mattered. You will find that she is awake, she responds to conversation. But she sits as though she were . . . It is as if she is absent from the room."

"And the cause?" Watson asked.

Simmons shook his head and said nothing.

Giving a quiet knock at the door, we entered the room. Listless and seated deep within an armchair, Mrs. Jones sat in the corner and took no note of our entering. A dimmed lamp sat upon the table at her side, the fire on the hearth nothing but warm coals. She was dressed for morning. She, in fact, still had on hat and cape.

"May we have light?" Watson whispered.

"She has forbidden us to touch anything," Simmons whispered back. "Said the darkness was perfectly acceptable to her."

"It suited her, was what she said," King offered. "And though she sits as you see there, she was fierce as a lion when we tried to draw the curtains."

"Good evening, Mrs. Jones." Watson approached the patient, summoning a warm smile as he did so. "I have been called in by these gentlemen here, and do believe I was expected.

That gentleman there is my colleague, Mr. Holmes. How are you feeling?"

In answer, Mrs. Jones shuddered and turned her hollow gaze to the doctor.

"I am cold," she said.

"Well, now. Cold may be remedied one way or another." Watson knelt at her side. He eyed me. "If you could be so kind as to draw the curtains and stir the fire? This room needs cheer as much as it needs warmth. This lamp. May I . . . ?"

Again, Mrs. Jones' listless, haunting gaze swept over Watson. "Cheer. I may never have cheer again, Doctor."

Simmons, King, and I quietly moved about, setting the room to rights, they with their bland practicality and I choosing my tasks so as to gather what information I may. Inwardly, I thanked Watson for having the foresight to assign me the hearth. No burnt fragments of diary entries lay amongst the embers. Whatever had so disturbed Mrs. Jones was not easily discovered in the room —thank heavens—or recently destroyed, unless she had had more presence of mind than currently.

"Have you any particular complaint, madam?" Watson kept his voice low and soothing. Removing his stethoscope from his hat, he gestured with it. "If I may?"

Mrs. Jones shifted and said nothing.

"Fine, fine, all fine," Watson could be heard

muttering throughout his gentle examination. He rose and beckoned.

We took our little grouping out into the hallway. Simmons stood so that he could see Mrs. Jones through the open door. Watson kept his voice low as he asked, "I do believe she is merely experiencing a shock. Has she said anything which might be pertinent to that? Do either of you know if Mrs. Jones has received any displeasing or disquieting news? Has anything happened for good or ill amongst the Order?"

Simmons eyes flicked to me, an unconscious gesture which his companion, King, noted.

"I earlier alluded to the recent misfortune with regards to Mr. Winter," King explained, his eyes hard and glittering like diamonds. "His malady was, shall we say, something private amongst our circle."

"He may be trusted with the truth," Watson vouched, steadfastly looking to King rather than Simmons. Inwardly my brain sounded danger. If Simmons wished my inquiry into the case to remain unknown to King, that chance had all but passed.

"Come, Watson, my presence here is unexpected. Far be it from me to force a confidence. Particularly when the lady appears to be fine and merely in need to quiet care from whatever has disturbed her," I offered. "If I may, I will bid you all a good evening."

It was King who accompanied me down to the

door to see me out. I could feel the energy in the man, the wound spring, the dynamic, magnetizing power which Watson had attempted to describe to me. I found it a wonder that Simmons remained the leader of their sect rather than King.

Standing together on the step while I craned my neck in search of a cab, I could feel King wishing to speak but not finding an opening. I created one for him. "What might someone gain by attacking someone else's astral persona?"

"Murder without leaving a mark upon your victim, without having stepped anywhere near the body? Leaving your enemy dead of seemingly natural causes behind a locked door within their own house—peaceful and secure within their own bed!—with nary a clue? I cannot imagine why someone bent on mischief would do so," King commented drily, as aloof, as casual in his response as I had been in asking my impertinent question. "There'll be a cab for you, sir. It is good to have met you, Mr. Sherlock Holmes. It is nice to know that our acquaintance and neophyte, Dr. Watson, enjoys a friendship with the foremost champion of the law."

DIFFERENT TIME,
DIFFERENT PERSON

CHAPTER 11

I resolved to call upon Mrs. Jones the next day, what with Watson having stayed late and, upon his return home, given his grim prognosis. "She has had a shock, and she is frail. And I cannot help but feel, Holmes, that we have not done enough for her, what with this other case nosing in, what with all your cases nosing in."

"I've done what I can with the evidence," had been my reply.

"Clearly there is new evidence."

Clearly.

I was doing what I could. And Watson was doing what he must. Mrs. Jones was experiencing acute distress. Any more strain and she might fail altogether. I could only hope that my presence would be a source of comfort, if for no other reason than that we might speak freely over what distressed her so.

As I say, Watson was doing his part. He had

assured me that, per unrelated discussions with King and Simmons, all able members of their theosophical group would be gathered at their hall this morning on some ceremony or other. And so I rode to Hill Street, alone save for my thoughts, which were noisome enough.

Mrs. Jones was much as I had left her. Sombre, stoic, and wrapped in a blanket, she sat with her gaze to the hearth. She was as a caged animal whose pen had been left open. Freed, but unaware of or unwilling to grasp that freedom. Unmoving, she allowed me to pass through her space as I gave a cursory glance to the blazing fire and then claimed the chair opposite her own.

"Mrs. Jones," I began.

"Why? Why should anyone wish me to suffer so?" she whispered. "I cannot sleep. Food is ash in my mouth. I fear every small thing. In every stranger's glance, an accusation. And all because of these accursed diary pages."

Mrs. Jones gave a low, throaty chuckle. "I'm going mad, Mr. Holmes. Mad with misery. Mad with fear and guilt. Mad with the efforts to try to reconcile with the fact that I do not remember writing these, and yet here they are! Positive proof in my hand."

"You are not going mad, no," I soothed, encouraged by the lady's having spoken with any energy at all. Her spark was unquenched if dimmed. "As you say, you have the physical proof in hand, Mrs. Jones. Physical proof with something akin to truth behind the story these pages proclaim. Which makes it blackmail. To what end and by whose hand I have yet to discover. No person with your best interests at heart would deliver this message in this way if they meant you well."

"Wrong, detective. Wrong and wrong again," she groaned. "In the desk there. Top drawer. I have here the key."

I accepted the key and, opening the desk, cast my eyes over the latest of the accursed diary pages. It was the same as its predecessors. It advanced the narrative but a tiny bit and contained nothing more inflammatory than evidence of an affair which my client claimed could not actually hurt her prospects or position. Why such a visceral reaction this time? I took the page and its envelope over to the window and examined it in better light. I frowned.

This, too, was the same as the one before. Only—I sucked in a breath—only there had been a minor correction made to the address. One penned by a hand which differed from the original writer.

"Neither Simmons nor King knows of this blackmail, Mrs. Jones?" I asked, returning to her side and trying my best to rein in my excitement.

"No," came the listless response.

"You are absolutely certain?"

Tears sprang to the corners of Mrs. Jones' eyes. She whispered, "I would sell my soul to keep

Simmons from the knowledge. And King? I would die of shame if he knew of it."

She turned glittering eyes towards me, half-smiling. "Simmons I have loved with all the passion of youth. But Frederick King . . . My soul loves King. He is my heart's master. I know I cannot be counted amongst Percy's theosophists. But King, he allows me to sup from those forbidden waters. He has been fairer to me than . . . I owe him."

We sat in silence for several moments, contemplating the fire. "If I may take this latest mailing with me, Mrs. Jones. I would like to make certain comparisons with that which you have already given over to my safekeeping."

She nodded silently and with nary a flicker of emotion in her wan face. The clouds had come back over the sun, and the window for our speaking freely had passed for the time being. I saw myself out.

Back at Baker Street, I updated Watson on the case and spent some time checking and double-checking both envelopes one against the other. At length, I double-checked myself, turning to my companion to ask, "What do you make of this, Watson?"

Taking up both papers, he peered close. "They appear to be of the same hand, written on the same stationery. Even the pen seems to have performed the same way. Were they—? No, that is too strange an idea."

"Go on," I encouraged, sensing that Watson had hit upon the same conclusion as I.

"These were not written at the same time, were they?" Watson frowned and looked to me. "Why bother making out several at once? Surely the risk increases with the more evidence a person accumulates, particularly when the recipient could then compare the one against the other so easily. Had Mrs. Jones saved the previous envelopes, for example . . ."

"Why indeed," I said. "If true, it would beg the question: how many are left in the blackmailer's possession? Are these prepared and sitting around in someone's study?"

"And how might we determine whose?" he continued.

"You see that correction there on the more recent of the two." I pointed.

"Where the word 'Road' was corrected to 'Street'?"

"Different pen. Different hand."

"Different time. Different person!" Watson concluded. "By Jove, the blackmailer has erred in making a correction on this one. Mrs. Jones— perhaps on a level she, herself, cannot identify— knows her tormenter. Hence the new breakdown of her nerves. Some subconscious note has been sounded in her."

I smiled grimly. "I have a theory."

THERE CAN BE NO GOING HALF-WAY

CHAPTER 12

I had told Watson I had a theory. What I hadn't told him was of what said theory was comprised. He was used to such reticence from me, of course, and had not pressed when I had lapsed into a moody smoke shortly thereafter. I had my thesis. Now I must collect the answers which yet remained out of reach. The first of such answers were promised to me in a knock on our door and the delivery of the afternoon mail.

It was my turn to call upon Mr. Turner. Rather, it might more accurately be termed that I had been summoned, per my having left my card for him and subsequently having received an invitation to follow up our initial interview. I set off at once.

"Your sustained interest is to your credit, Mr. Holmes," Turner said, welcoming me into his home. I took the offered seat. He looked me over, a curious half-smile playing about his lips. "You have passed the examination."

"Examination?"

That same half-smile broadened, and Mr. Turner's eyes twinkled. "Ah. What day was it we met? I happened upon two of our society that afternoon who were more than willing to test our new initiate. You would not have been aware of the scrutiny, of course. Or known it for what it was. Such things come with knowledge."

He leaned forward in his chair. "And you are ready for such knowledge."

"If you will have me." Shifting in my seat, I matched him in intensity, only obliquely conscious that I did so. It was as though other forces were at work in the room. Other wills than my own. How many mysteries might I find amongst these secretive sorcerers?

"There can be no going about this half-way." Somehow Turner broke the space between us. Without having moved, he seemed to shrink away upon having spoken the stern injunction. I could feel the offer being rescinded, and inwardly, I scrambled about in an attempt to make myself attractive and suitable to their purposes once more.

My logical self resisted the abasement. In sending Watson to Winter's house alone at the outset of our case, I had inadvertently placed myself in the position of having to apply to the likes of Turner for my theosophical explorations.

My cowardice in the face of my inconvenient interest in Simmons' order had produced unexpected fruit in Watson's subsequent inclusion within our client's acquaintances. At least until I had blundered into things through the misinterpretation of a telegram.

"I am unaccustomed to doing things by halves," I explained to my host. "And I should have no trouble in keeping confidential what is entrusted to me of your society's practices."

Private concerns would remain private concerns. My spiritual struggles would find resolution without Watson having known of my having sought assuagement. Perhaps I might even enlighten him, in time.

No, I would not come into the Society of Universal Energies—nor any other—upon my knees. My steady gaze to Turner might have said more than my words for he nodded, apparently satisfied.

"You shall dedicate a space for mystic and theosophic purposes. Then, Mr. Holmes, you shall commit a great deal to memory. This from manuscripts from which you shall be bound to share not one iota of what you have learned unless it be in direct service to our society and without the public's knowledge."

"I understand." I made the solemn promise. I paused, making sure that I still had Turner's attention, and then added, "Are there any dangers I need be aware of?"

"Dangers, Mr. Holmes?" My question appeared to spark some mirth in him. I, a man who routinely set myself up against the lowest villains and made brutal enemies of dangerous men, afraid of a little magic?

He said, "There are always dangers to what anyone does, Mr. Holmes. It may be dangerous for a person to cross a street. But to your question, yes, there have been rare incidents."

"Such as?"

Narrowing his eyes at me, Turner's testing gaze signalled to me that I had pushed too hard. Still, he said, "We have lost two members in the fifteen years that I have had the privilege of leading the Society of Universal Energies. The first was an historically unhappy man. His membership amongst our sect was an error. The second we lost but two years back. He did not follow our rules. Indulgence was his weakness and his downfall.

"But I can see from your consulting detective's tendency for suspicion that you've more questions to follow this first. Let me answer those before you ask them," said he. "Would I ascribe these losses to malevolence? No. This world—and others through which we may travel—requires chaos. It requires bitter failures and unhappy events. But we don't hunt them all down and prosecute simply because we don't like that something terrible happened. We—I, Mr. Holmes, have lost two members. But that is life, is it not?"

He had tested me. I still had tests aplenty for him, though I should tread more carefully now. I asked, "And if I find that I am unable to fulfil my promise to the Society? Say through some defect in character or moral fibre? Am I . . . ?"

"Are you free to leave with what secret knowledge you have gained prior to that point?" This time, Mr. Turner's smile was genuine if sad. "I believe it is an honest and humble heart which asks such questions, and so, yes, you would no longer be counted amongst our company. If I passed you on the street, you would pass as though a stranger to me. But you would have my friendship. In here." Turner indicated, with a touch to his breast, his own honest and humble heart.

I quailed. I was not one given to abdication. But the handing off of personal responsibility, the duty to a higher power—any power outside myself —had become like a drug to me. And this without my having felt its effects first hand. For a man feeling guilty, feeling secretly unworthy, this was clemency without confession, and if I were to move forward in my life at all, I must have it.

GAMES AND TRICKS

CHAPTER 13

Days later saw me renewing my acquaintanceship with King. He, Simmons, Watson, and myself were meeting to have dinner with two other gentlemen. It was Simmons who had issued the invitation, but it was King, we were told, who had chosen the party. Both Mr. Edward James and Mr. Thomas Carter were unknown to us.

We had hardly been seated, with introductions made, when King looked to me from across the table and said, "Mr. Holmes, I hadn't had the pleasure the other evening of experiencing your little trick."

" 'Tis a game more suited to parlours than public houses, Mr. King," Simmons cautioned. "Surely you don't mean to test our friend so openly."

"I do mean to," King said unswervingly, his eyes locking to my own. "Myself and these two gentlemen here, James and Carter. You may skip over Simmons, as he apparently does not wish such scrutiny on himself."

"There is often so little that I may say to gentlemen such as yourselves," I deflected, my voice low. "What without current professions leaving impressions upon your clothing, fingers, or wrists. I say current. Mr. Carter is a former ship's surgeon. Aboard a whaler, if I had to guess. You had a son who followed in your footsteps, Mr. Carter. You have my sincere condolences on his not returning home. As for Mr. King, you have been in London for several years now. Your home-coming from a failed lecture post in Vienna was—"

"What devilry is this?" Carter growled, half-rising.

"Sit. Down," King hissed, his eyes still on me as he absently toyed with a silver teaspoon, playing so that it caught the light. "Go on, Mr. Holmes. Tell us something you cannot guess by the coin on a man's watch chain or the shape of his lapels. Something abstruse. Something . . . secret."

This time it was Mr. James who had gained his feet. Only the man did not appear to have chosen his actions. Staggering backwards, he clawed at the air in front of him. His chair crashed to the ground.

"It's his heart. Quick, man!" Watson shouted to Simmons who had stepped back from the flailing Mr. James.

Eyes wild, his hands seeming to grapple some invisible assailant, Mr. James let out a slivery, shivery sort of moan. He continued to careen this way and that, forcing the other diners nearby to gasp in alarm or voice muttered complaints.

"Grab him. Get him out of here." This time, Watson practically shoved Simmons towards James. Between him and myself, we managed to grab hold of the man and manoeuvre him towards the doorway. Carter and King made their apologies in our wake.

Mr. James shook us off in the doorway of the restaurant and nearly tumbled down the stairs onto the pavement. His flailing had become convulsions. This was no heart failure.

"He's having a fit. Somebody help him!" Simmons cried.

King leapt forward, receiving a mighty blow from James' fists as he did so. Between Carter's strength and my dexterity, we managed to subdue poor Mr. James. Watson had disappeared during the short fracas. He returned from inside the restaurant and handed off a wine cork, instructing, "Between his teeth if you can manage it. And get his collar loosened and his tie off."

A trickle of blood leaked from the corner of Mr. James' mouth, evidence that his gnashing had already done some harm. Without warning, he went limp in our hands.

"He has lost his fight," King pronounced, his voice practically a whisper.

"He lives," Watson countered.

"Here now, what is this disturbance?" The local PC shouldered his way into our tight knot. With quick eyes, he assessed the situation. Seeing Watson crouched at the man's side, noting the doctor's hat with its stethoscope, he added, "Ah, you've a doctor already then. I'll see about this crowd. You there, whistle a cab. There's a gentleman here taken ill. Clear out. Give the man room to breathe."

Mr. James' eyes fluttered open. Both Carter and I had loosed our hold on him, and so freed, the man jumped to his feet, spat out the cork, and with a wild shout, took off at a run down the street.

"Good heavens!" Watson sputtered, having fallen backward in his surprise. Mr. King proved as spry as his energetic personality would suggest. He was gone, along with a trailing Mr. Carter, in a matter of moments. The two men shouted to their friend to slow his steps and heed their call.

"Let him go, Mr. Holmes." Simmons' hand was on my shoulder. He shook his head gravely. "As King says, Mr. James has lost his fight. King will know it himself soon enough. Come, let us go back to Baker Street where I can discuss more freely the import of these terrible events."

.   .   .

"It was a spectacle. Had he known I was in attendance, I doubt he'd have been so bold with his actions," Simmons moaned.

"Who him?" Watson frowned.

"Him. Him!" Simmons cried. "Our unseen enemy. The devil which besets my flock. The crowd protected me; protected my aura from being felt by him, singled out. Perhaps it is for the better that he made his error so publicly. But poor Mr. James. Poor, poor Mr. James. Soon as I realized what was happening to the man I made a sign —I had to protect myself, after all—and concentrated my vision on Mr. James and his assailant. The other folk present, they missed out on the fight to end all fights."

Simmons' eyes shown. Speaking animatedly, he paced the carpet at 221B, slapping his hands along the back of the couch for emphasis at varied intervals. It was the most palpable I had seen the man. It was as though James' weakening had strengthened our client. Iron hard and wholly excited, he continued, "The fight for a soul; nay, the fight for control of the baser stuff without which we have no connection to this world. No tangible one, anyhow. I've paid to see my fair share of Maiden Lane spars. This fight, though. This fight. I could well-nigh see the two spirits grappling in the air above poor Mr. James. He hadn't wanted to separate, I am sure, and so hadn't true control over either his physical or his double self. It was panic plain and plain."

"You saw Mr. James' astral self?" Watson asked, agog and wholly sceptical. I was glad for my friend's question, for it meant that I did not have to voice it and could continue my scrutiny of our client's remarkable vitality uninterrupted.

Simmons paused his zealous pacing. He cocked his head as if listening. "No. No, I did not. But I know the signs. You could smell the ozone as each fought for dominance in the body. Poor Mr. James."

I had not smelled this so-called ozone. What I had witnessed, however, had been distinctly unpleasant and carried within it the scent of theatre. Someone had put on a performance for our little audience of five. Four, if I considered that one amongst the company was the play-wright. And I had a fairly good idea of who.

I asked, "You mentioned the fairly fantastical 'silver cord' which tethers the soul to the body. In the fight we witnessed tonight, what happens to said silver cord if an astral spirit invades someone else's physical body? Presumably, the old is severed and a new cord is made?"

Simmons opened his mouth and then closed it. Thoughtful, he thumbed his chin and made a show of muttering to himself. "I would have to consult our texts. Yes. That one is beyond me, Mr. Holmes. Goodness, how is it I never considered such a dilemma? Perhaps King would know . . ."

"I would, at this juncture, not confide in Mr. King, Mr. Simmons," I muttered.

"You do not mean to say . . . ?" Simmons' mouth hung open. He shook his head. "No, I won't hear of it. You've met the man. Watson?"

The appeal was turned back to me by my partner. "Holmes?"

I sighed, disliking the requirement that I proceed here and now before I had acquired all of my evidence—acquired, in fact, any hard evidence. I spoke, "What is the nature of the relationship between Mrs. Jones and Mr. King?"

"I beg your pardon!"

"What do you know of Mr. Frederick King from three years ago?" I pressed. "Four? Ten?"

"His references were sound. His education—"

"Perfectly suited for inclusion in your order, yes, yes." I waved off Simmons' indignance. "And perfectly suited to acquiring the trust of impressionable female protégés who are barred entry into your little club."

"How dare you, sir."

"How dare I?" I rose from my chair. "I dare because you asked me to look into your case. And what I have found is a man amongst your close acquaintances who has a history of different names in different cities, in different orders, sects, and societies."

"What is your proof?" Simmons challenged. "You and your unbelieving, practical, earth-bound logical self must have proof. Produce it, then. I'll wait."

"For that I would have to—"

"You've nothing," Simmons spat. "You've bias. You've a preconceived idea of what is real, what is right, what can and cannot be."

"Now, see here, Mr. Simmons," Watson began.

But Simmons would not hear what either of us had to say. Incensed, he gathered up both hat and coat and, with an impassioned, "Good day to you both," he left.

BELIEFS, CONVICTIONS, AND QUESTIONS

CHAPTER 14

"Well, I never!" Watson stared agog out the window, looking down on Simmons' retreating form.

"I challenged a great many things for him and all at once," I lamented, watching alongside Watson. "His beliefs, his trust in his lieutenant, his regard—or, at the least, his former regard—for Mrs. Jones. I ought to have anticipated such an outcome."

"You could not well have let him go on, ranting and fanatical over this soul fight which he claims to have seen."

"Perhaps he did see it," I countered. "I do believe Simmons wholeheartedly believes everything he says to us. And though it does not match our experiences, it does not make the belief any less real. I ought not have challenged him. Or, rather, I should have done so more carefully."

"You fear he will run straight to King with your accusations," Watson said.

I turned to him in surprise. "No, I do not believe he will, actually. And if he did, what would be the risk in it? King knows I am on to him."

"Hence the demonstration at the restaurant tonight," Watson gruffed.

"That was for Simmons as much as it was for you and me," I acknowledged. "Our wicked magician knows that, with me on his trail, his days living in London as Mr. Frederick King are numbered. Thus, he is buying himself time. Buying himself time to take the leap to a new life. Take up a new name in a new city using his old tricks."

I broke off my statement to scribble off several quick telegrams and rang the bell.

"And to what end?" Watson cried.

I did not answer. I had no answer as of yet.

The door to our sitting room opened, and I said, "Mrs. Hudson, could you see that these go out to their intended parties? Thank you."

Together, Watson and I sat in silence for long minutes, the nighttime around us growing stiller and stiller and the hearth fire shrinking lower and lower.

"Perhaps I am wrong, and Simmons will run to his friend as you say," I mused, gazing unseeing into the glowing mass of coals beneath the grate. "In which case, what would it matter? What would any of it matter? No. No, any answer is but illusion. The facts fanciful at best."

At length Watson yawned. "I am still of the opinion that Simmons is as suspect—perhaps even more so—than King. Simmons was the one engaged to Miss Overweg and at a time period which predates King living in London. It was Simmons who had a dalliance with the wife of his best friend. It is members of Simmons' order that suffer in this whole affair. His temper just now? What if our master magician has, all along, meant for me to meet King and for you to persecute the man? It could be that the latter's only crime has been in keeping silent while he has had his eye on someone whose power, literal and otherwise, may cause real harm."

He rose. "Well, I am off to bed. Good night, Holmes."

Alone and sitting motionless in my chair beside the cold fire, I considered Watson's words.

It could be Simmons. It absolutely could be Simmons. He was intelligent, and he was undoubtedly dedicated to the beliefs which ran so strangely through the case he had brought to my attention. It was this case which made his order's ideologies manifest. Something had caused deaths, caused chaos, caused ripples outside of a closed and private hall of limited membership. Why not magic? Simmons wanted secrecy, and yet he needed openness if his Theosophical Order of Odic Forces was to have any impact upon the world at all, if it were to continue, to thrive.

If, for example, Simmons had anticipated the possibility of my involvement in Mrs. Jones' case, he could have arranged to have a case of his own that I would never, ever, take up. Or perhaps he would have a hope that I should give up said investigation the more occult, magical, and spiritual it became. Simmons could well be a talented performer. He had to be in his special calling—his profession, as he had called it. King could be another blockade, another trick; someone Simmons had invited into his order, into his life, so as to shield his activities through King's less than clean history.

Thinking of King, of the patchwork history of this restless, itinerant magician which I had learned in part from Mr. Turner through further careful side inquiries, made me think of Turner and his Society of Universal Energies. He was an intelligent, learned man. His order, and others, was populated by judges and gentlemen, physicians and poets, men who held government posts. By the likes of Mr. Frederick King, who had bounded from one to the other until he had settled within Simmons' group some three-plus years ago.

The rolls were the educated, the dreamers, the monied, the fervent. Who was I to say they were all of them, any of them, misguided? For I hoped, I dreamed and hoped, the same as them. Nay, I needed. I needed there to be more to this life than conflict and greed and betrayal and humanity's basest impulses set against some artificial morality. I was coming to believe that we all did and that my burning was nothing special or ruinous if I could but find my answers. And Simmons had come to my doorstep knowing this, promising peace to my soul without ever being aware he had even done so.

I pictured Simmons in my mind's eye. The man standing on the carpet of 221B, twisting his hat in his hand. I recalled his anxious fervour as he proclaimed the existence of true and identifiable evil in our world. The existence of such organizations as the Theosophical Order of Odic Forces.

Odic Forces. My research had informed me that these were the life force or spirit. A thing which bore striking resemblance to the astral self and something which lived at the heart of Simmons' case. Odic Forces. Named for the god Odin some fifty years prior by Baron Carl von Reichenbach.

Reichenbach.

Reichenbach.

Reichenbach.

Evil.

Evil.

Moriarty.

Who I had killed. Whose death I had hoped to cause.

And I had been rewarded with life. Life and

guilt and questions. I had known, in 221B, in fleeing to the Continent with Watson, in standing on that cliff's edge, what I stood for and why. I had been certain of my principles, my righteousness. With respect to Moriarty, the lines were perfectly clear. Until, in an instant, my mind had asked if that were true. When I looked into the living eyes of a man who I was actively seeking to kill, I had admitted to uncertainty, to the idea that one might never know and that that might be where evil truly lives. My disgrace had only deepened when, within that same hour, I had denied Watson, denied life, even while I secretly clung to both with a fierce desperation that can only be termed love. I, the unworthy Sherlock Holmes, had been given a second chance, and I hadn't the faintest idea how to move forward within it.

I had since come to find that I had hopes. The promises and wisdom held by orders such as Simmons' and Turner's were either kept alive by hope or kept hope alive. The logical step had been to determine which it was.

I had read early on that to set one's astral self outside the physical body, one must have a calm mind, a stillness of soul. I had no such stillness. I had no peace. As I say, I had been granted life, and for three years I had run from this gift. What was I to do with it? I was done. My work complete! My vengeance and anger spent! I did not want the subsequent responsibility of having to live.

What was I to do now, save work off the debt of guilt which seemed to grow rather than fade with each passing day? London, a cage. My profession, a burden. Watson—

Watson, a regular reminder of how much I had wronged him. A reminder of how good a man he must be to simply take my return and bury his grief in his joy. To never say one single word of reproof, or hold any of my actions—my three years of a perfect and cruel lie—against me.

The hours of my sitting and trying to wrest my soul from my body passed as might a restless sleeper's turning about in bed. No headway was made save for frustration, and the day had begun to throw its light around the edges of 221B's curtains before it occurred to me to arise and take myself off to sleep.

I was still in the cane chair by the cold hearth when the maid came in to build the fire and deliver the morning's paper. I eyed the proceedings through slitted lids, unmoving, and snatched at the paper as soon as I was alone. I had spent the night in airy, querulous contemplation and required the anchor of the morning *Times* to bring me back into the realm of fact and materiality. The soothing solidity of the heavy black print brought me earthbound once more.

A headline toward the bottom of the second page had me on my feet and ringing for Mrs.

151

Hudson. Opening the door, I hurried to wake Watson.

He cracked a groggy eye at me, and said, "Goodness, Holmes. What is the matter?"

"Mr. Edward James has committed suicide." I shook the paper in my hand in emphasis.

"The Mr. Edward James of last night's excitement? Our Mr. James?"

" 'Shocking Suicide Leads to Incidental Solving of No Less than Six Burglaries,' " I read. " 'In the early hours of morning, a man jumped from the railway viaduct onto Dockley Road in an apparent suicide, per witness statements. Victim has been identified as Mr. Edward James who, friends report, had suffered some type of disturbance of mind at a restaurant earlier in the evening. A note was found at his house amongst his effects alongside several pieces of evidence connecting him to no less than six outstanding burglaries—some evidence going back some two years.'

"If it isn't our James, the incident at the restaurant certainly bears striking resemblance, does it not?" I asked.

"I will get dressed at once," Watson promised.

"I rang Mrs. Hudson for coffee," I said. "If we could leave by half past the hour, I will be satisfied that we have not missed all."

"Holmes." Watson finally noted my own state. "Have you slept at all?"

I ignored him. "We leave in forty minutes."

JUMP

CHAPTER 15

We arrived on the scene to find one of Gregson's men guarding the site from the curious and the morbid thrill seeker. Recognizing my companion and me, he waved and stepped to the side in invitation.

"Mr. William, how is your family?" Watson held out a hand.

"I had not been informed you were coming, detective," he said. "Good to see you, Dr. Watson. All is well."

PC William gestured to the street and to the elevated arches above. "Poor devil landed there; and fell from there."

"May we?" I asked, looking upward.

"Be my guest, Mr. Holmes, but there'll be nothing left to see now that the body has been taken away and witnesses have said their piece," he said.

Minutes later, Watson and I stood upon the

elevated platform. With lens in hand, I examined the stones of the balustrade then turned to look downward to where Mr. James had met his end. A large patch stained the dark wood of the street darker still. The echo of spilt blood and much of it.

"Holmes?" A hand on my arm called me out of my thoughts.

"Hmm?" Blinking, I shook off the memory which had imposed itself over the scene, that of a fresh crimson stain on wet rock, the spray of a tumbling waterfall working slowly, but efficiently, to wash away the evidence of a death.

Watson followed my gaze downward to the street below. When I did not speak nor hurry to look away, he glanced at me. On his face: inquiry laced with worry. Quietly he asked, "What is it, Holmes?"

"It is a horrible way for a man to die," I said simply. "Come. Let us see what Constable William has to tell."

The policeman shook his head at our approach, saying, "It's a suicide plain and plain, Mr. Holmes. You've the evidence of the scene, and we've a credible witness. May I ask why you are taking such an interest? Is it the burglaries? Those are plain and plain as well."

Watson stepped forward. "We were with Mr. James at dinner last night, and I was the doctor on the scene who tried to treat Mr. James for his distressing fit. Medically speaking, that gives me more than a little interest in satisfying for myself how all of this happened."

"If it were anybody else." William frowned. "But, you've helped satisfy us every now and again on a little point here and there. Witnesses report Mr. James jumped off the bridge and onto the street below. Medically speaking, the distress of the man's mind was apparent in the way he was behaving in the minutes leading to his death. Two men who stood down here, edge of the road, said they thought him playing a game the way he led on. It was like a child's game. Jumping up and down. On one foot. Then the other. Then Mr. James went up on the edge. And that is when the station clerk became involved. I can provide his address. Rail company sent him home on account of his nerves. They've someone else working Spa Road today."

Thanking William, I jotted two addresses— that of the witness and the victim—upon my cuff. Together, Watson and I rode for the district wherein the Spa Road booking clerk, a Mr. Graff, lived.

We introduced ourselves, and Mr. Graff gestured that we come inside. "I've made my statement to the police, but if there's more to be got out of this horrid business by you gentlemen with my saying what I saw, I'll say my piece again."

"If you could start at the beginning, Mr. Graff," I said.

"I've been a booking clerk for nigh on eight

155

years. We see all sorts of hooliganism from all sorts. Some at the station. Some along the rail. So when I saw a man stumbling along the edge of the raised platform in the dark, I thought it a drunk, and I went to get him down. Then I saw he was not alone. There was a man there. Talking to him. The other man told me to stay back, stay back and get the police, get help. Said that this was his friend and that the man had threatened to jump—"

Here, Graff ceased to speak, and trembling violently, he passed his hands over his eyes.

"Mr. Graff?" I prompted.

"That man was talking to his friend the whole time. A low voice. Reasonable and friendly-like. I did as asked. I made to return to my station, thinking to call for help but— But, God help me, I turned back around. Something about it made me uneasy. I could hear the other man talking more urgently to his friend, and I—" Graff swayed in his chair. "And then that poor man jumped."

"The man, the man who had been talking to him. What of him? What did he do when his friend jumped? What did he say?"

"I looked around and just didn't see him. I was so shocked, understand. I, and anyone else awake, was looking at the man who killed himself." Graff's voice shook. "I didn't want to think of him. I just kept thinking of that poor soul lying in the road."

"You say you had an uneasy feeling," I pressed.

Graff closed his eyes. Twin tracks of tears rolled down the man's face as he admitted, "I'd swear to all that's holy that the man who warned me off his friend . . . When he said the word 'jump,' it hadn't sounded like something a friend would say. It sounded encouraging-like. Cold-blooded. More a command than anything else. But that couldn't be right. Tell me I heard him wrong, else I'll be haunted by man's cruelty all my days."

"There was a note found amongst the victim's effects. Last night, you did your very best to save the life of a man who was set upon his own destruction. If that doesn't speak to the goodness of man, I don't know what else would," Watson assured. "I've seen battle, Mr. Graff. And I will tell you that I have heard the strangest, most damning things while the stress of a moment has each second pass as though it were an hour. A baby's cry upon a battlefield, the ringing of a bell. Our senses do strange things when our minds and hearts most wish us to be elsewhere and hard reality other than what it is."

Graff nodded, and our impassioned interview came to a close.

We hailed a cab to Mr. James' home.

"I put him there, Watson. I put Mr. Edward

James in pieces in Dockley Road," I murmured my hollow, defeated complaint, drawing my fingers down over my face and heaving a sigh. Leaning back against the cab's seat, I shook my head, my enervation rendering the gesture as small and futile as I currently felt. "I was too late to realize the danger. Ha; I never thought of the danger! I considered Mr. James an accomplice rather than a victim."

Watson said not a word.

In gaining access to Mr. James' home, we encountered even less resistance from the PC on guard there than we had at the scene of the tragedy. He knew us, though I did not recognise him. Gregson's name bandied about secured us a tour of the police findings.

"Suicide note. And written in the man's hand. Easily confirmed by the other private correspondence. Sealed up in this envelope here and left upon his desk," the policeman said. "Safe was open and contained evidence of seven different unsolved burglaries dating back to '92. We're concluding that this Mr. James wanted to come clean of his crimes and left things so that we didn't have to force our way into any discoveries."

I frowned and, upon applying my lens and the light of a strong lamp to the scene, concluded that the safe had not been forced. Similar scrutiny had me concluding that nobody had entered or exited Mr. James' house by unusual or clandestine means. Turning to the desk and Mr. James' final correspondence with the wide world, I read the note, examined the paper upon which it had been written, the envelope within which it had been discovered, and ran my fingertips over the various personal effects nearby for good measure. Frowning, I eyed the note again and asked, "This is how this was found? Just as I see here?"

Our host gestured brusquely. "Mr. James kept a nice and tidy desk for the most part, as you can see. The note lay there. Right in the centre. Not uncommon for folks who've chosen as Mr. James did. They've left the note. They want to ensure it is read."

"This note," I said. "The one which reads 'I confess. I confess before all in this earth and beyond who hold the power to judge mankind. And in unburdening my heart, I find that even now I tremble at what dishonest and indecent things I have had the compulsion to do.' Etc. and so forth. This note, sealed inside this envelope."

"Yes." More exasperation from the policeman. Watson looked from him to me, troubled for all the trouble I seemed intent on causing.

"With today's date upon it?" I asked again.

The PC's glance seemed to say that he was quite surprised to think at how I could in any way be famous for my detective skills.

Undeterred, I pressed, "And you believe this reads like a suicide note rather than as a written confession by a man who intended to live, having thus cleared his conscience?"

"It doesn't matter what I believe. It's not as if we can go ask Mr. James what he meant by it, Mr. Holmes! It is our task to observe and interpret what was obviously the careful, precise, and premeditated final actions of a man who took his own life early this morning."

"Mmm." Head down, I tapped the desktop lightly. "It just doesn't have the right flavour. I should know, I've read several—and penned two— over the course of my career."

"Mayhap the man quailed from setting it down directly. It's near enough to satisfy us," the policeman cried. His exasperation had reached its peak.

"Near enough." I snorted. Our quick and fruitless investigation concluded, Watson and I thanked the man and made for home.

Back at Baker Street I allowed free rein to my anger. "I would say that it is a wonder that the police managed anything useful in my absence but for the fact that I have, clearly, been the greatest of asses myself!"

Pacing the rug, I nearly trod over Watson's feet twice in my rounds. "Miss Overweg's suicide. I ought to have pursued that from the first. But no, I listened to Simmons and his excuses. I could have prevented last night's tragedy, Watson. The Henry death? Miss Overweg and her pertinacious brother? It has bothered me from the first that my path was barred from investigating either, and instead of forcing the issue, I sat by and read books and considered how membership in Simmons' order might help me, and I did nothing."

"Help you?" Watson's inquiry rang sharp.

"Help me help Simmons," I snarled, taking up my chair at last and putting a coal to my cherrywood pipe.

"Mr. James did not kill himself." Watson waded tentatively into my foul temper. "I mean, he did kill himself. But it was not a suicide."

I would not be baited.

He continued, "And in the absence of your telling me how this is either true or false, I shall have to venture guesswork on my own."

"Ask yourself about the envelope, Watson," I muttered.

"The envelope," he repeated, puzzled.

"The envelope. For one, it's utterly ridiculous to seal away your suicide note and then leave your safe wide open."

"And your theory, Holmes?"

"Mr. James did not know what the envelope contained."

"The note was in his handwriting!" Watson ejaculated. "The other contents of his desk, his cabinet, his safe prove that fairly conclusively."

"As do the diary entries in Mrs. Jones' hand seemingly condemn her in her case. There is more," I said, rising. Going to my desk, I took up the evidence of Mrs. Jones' blackmailing case and passed both envelopes to my partner.

"This is . . ." His eyes scanned the papers. "These addresses are in James' writing."

"I saw the corresponding stationery in one of his pigeon holes."

Watson looked thunderstruck.

"Now you see why I am angry with myself for not having pursued, sooner, a line of investigation which might have helped us weeks back," I said, retaking my chair and pipe. "In the absence of any other admittance to the truth of things, I looked into what the official coroner's report had to say about Miss Overweg. What King told you about her death is true. The young woman died from rat poison. If, then, taking King's narrative as fact, I find it suggestive."

"Go on."

I sat forward. "Imagine, if you will, a young woman who has fallen under the thrall of a very accomplished magician. Imagine, too, that she—like others before her—will do most anything this magician commands. Now, imagine that, one night, the instruction is to take this harmless substance. Perhaps it is medicinal; perhaps commonplace food and drink."

"Now, we imagine that this young woman was very much alone and unable to receive timely medical help," Watson concluded miserably.

"And with Mr. James—it is but the work of a moment for a loss of balance or misstep to prove fatal, providing the height and situation are great enough, yes," I said. "Which leaves me one last exercise of the imagination: let us surmise that, by magician, I really mean a person of magnetic personality and a skillset which takes advantage of those who might put themselves in a position of deep suggestion."

"Auto-suggestion," Watson replied. "That would fit well with Mr. James' symptoms at dinner. By Heavens, Holmes, this villainous enemy is nothing more than a skilled hypnotist?"

"I would not paint King in so thin of strokes, but yes," I drawled.

"King!" Watson ejaculated. "So you still believe it him."

"I absolutely do," I said. "At dinner last evening, King's challenge to my little game of deductions came at me so that he might employ the most basic of stage magician's tricks. Misdirection. Look here. Not there. But I saw. I saw his playing with the polished teaspoon so that it would flicker and catch the light. Mr. James' gaze was fixed upon it, a moth to a flame. This the whole time that Simmons was . . . well, Simmons was Simmons. In fact, I doubt anyone save for myself and Mr. James observed the spoon."

"I had not, no. But even so, Holmes, hypnotism cannot make a person do anything that crosses certain moral lines. A hypnotised person cannot, say, be made to murder someone else or kill themselves," Watson cautioned. Thumbing his chin, he added, "But both suicides account for that fact and so have taken advantage of the element of surprise on their victim."

"And poor Mrs. Jones is only having a creative endeavour with an old guilty secret, yes, Watson!" I cried.

"This is diabolical."

"This is conjecture," I countered. "But I agree. We must send word to Simmons. He must go to Mrs. Jones and guard against King and whatever next he might do to anyone who has fallen under his power."

A ring of the front bell brought us both to our feet.

WARRANTS AND APOLOGIES

CHAPTER 16

"I must apologize to you, Mr. Holmes, Dr. Watson," Simmons began.

We had admitted our visitor with no small amount of self-conscious disquiet. It was as though our discussion had summoned him to our hearth rug. But our client's distress soon overtook any trepidation we might feel.

Simmons continued, "Your words to me yesterday evening angered me, Mr. Holmes. But you do not know the extent of why that would be unless I confessed all. I am prepared to do so now, as it might save me, might save other innocents under my shepherding, from further persecution.

"The night that King wrote requesting Watson's presence at Mrs. Jones' residence, I do not believe I gave any specifics as to why we had entrusted her care to Dr. Watson, but I am sure you surmised that it was connected to my case in no small way," Simmons said. "My acquaintance with Mrs. Jones, however, goes back further and is of a much more intimate nature than through a mere interest in theosophy. I do not mean to betray the lady's honour, but I fear that my presence in her life has put Mrs. Jones in danger, and it is my duty to disclose that which, otherwise, should have remained a secret. Your intimating that King might have some special place within her life roused more in me than anger that he might have allied himself to my cause under false pretences. It provoked the jealousy of a former lover. And it is with this confession that I beg you do all that you can to remove King from our lives if, indeed, he is as untrustworthy as you claim."

I blinked, nonplussed.

I said, "Mr. Simmons, do understand that my limitations lie in what I am legally allowed to do under the auspices of the law. I am no policeman. And, at present, I have nothing which would persuade a judge to sign off on a warrant against Mr. King."

"What would it take?" Simmons fell to his knees. "I will burgle his home. I will waylay him so that you might secure what you need to lay charges against him. Please, let me not find news of Mrs. Jones' death by suicide in tomorrow morning's paper."

"Come now." Watson helped Simmons to his feet and directed him to the couch. He pressed a cool glass into the occultist's hands and turned to me. "What would it take, Holmes?"

I considered. Then answered, "Have you a sample of his handwriting?"

"Something involving the word 'street'?" Watson added.

"The hall," Simmons answered. "We keep records. King had offered himself up as keeper, and so something of his would have to be written there."

"How long would this take you to retrieve?" I asked.

"I'll be back within the hour," he promised and was gone.

Simmons was as good as his word, and save for a stop at Mrs. Jones' per my suggestion, he returned to Baker Street without delay. He had with him a small notebook containing the names and addresses of his members, the more recent entries penned in a now-familiar hand. Additionally, he had thought to bring the booklet of telegram forms from which the summons to Watson had been written.

"Ah, carbonic paper. The detective's hero," I said, thumbing through to the copy which would serve our case.

We had not wasted our hour, either. Watson had returned to Mr. James' and, with some favours promised to Gregson in the future, was able to secure more samples of King's writing from his correspondence to his friend.

In our hands? A thin strand. But a strand all the same.

By evening, we were on the move. Though my allegiance in this case had been unofficially pledged to Inspector Gregson, it was his colleague and sometime professional rival, Detective Lestrade, who rode with us to King's residence.

"You've another strange series of happenstance to explain on this one, I am sure, Mr. Holmes," Lestrade said when met by our singular lack of details. Simmons had, of course, taken himself out of our company lest he somehow compromise our apprehension of the man who had systematically destroyed the lives of so many in Simmons' acquaintance. He would find us at Baker Street when the devil was hanged. His words, not mine.

Simmons had, in fact, expressed fears that the police would not be able to do anything to King—warrant or no.

"How can we stop a rogue magician?" he had cried. "His powers! They are too great. You simply cannot catch a magician bent on evil. He will do this again and again. He will go where he will and use his power as he sees fit. A new locale. New victims. The only way to stop a villain like him is a bullet."

Reminded again of my limits—we were neither judge nor jury—and the fact that murdering King would put Simmons in as legally treacherous a position, he bowed to reason and left us to our task.

Mr. Frederick King was arrested on the steps of his home.

Seeing me, seeing Watson, he sneered, "I ought to have expected as much the night you came snooping around to Hill Street. What you have won't hold in court. I'll never stand before a judge. You'll see!"

"You'll stand, Mr. King," Lestrade said, ushering the handcuffed man into the police vehicle. "You'll stand, and you'll find justice proclaiming you guilty or innocent."

ANSWERS

CHAPTER 17

"You'll want to know why I have done what I have, Mr. Holmes." King sat between two officers as we rode through the city, his wrists manacled but his posture impeccable and almost buoyant. I sat on the bench opposite, between Watson and Inspector Lestrade. King smirked, adding, "Not that I did it. But why."

Lestrade narrowed his gaze at the prisoner. "I am bound to warn you that anything you may say will appear in evidence against you."

"Oh, I confess." King shrugged. "I confess to the suicide of Mr. Edward James, Miss Eunice Overweg, Mr. William Henry . . . shall I continue, Mr. Holmes? Or were they the only people Mr. Simmons was concerned over?"

"Mrs. Jones," Watson growled.

King laughed. "Ah, Mrs. Jones and her

dangerous liaison with Mr. Simmons. Chronicled in her own hand."

Lestrade shot King a disgusted look.

"Do let him continue," I drawled. "The puzzle of a blackmailer who makes no demands and merely tortures his victim has engaged my curiosity for some weeks now."

King grinned. "I did what I did to Mrs. Jones for the fun of it, Mr. Holmes. For the power."

He lifted his manacled wrists. "Surely you know the thrill of having unequivocal power over another human. The more Mrs. Jones struggled with her guilty secret, the more it drove her into my arms. She needed a confessor. Her soul cried out for reconciliation. I purify through my fire. I unearth the secrets which keep people from true peace and burn their shame from their souls."

"And why is it they disclose their deepest secrets to you, of all people?" Watson positively sparked with rage.

"Have any of you gentlemen a mirror upon you? A shining, polished coin, perhaps? I work best with a candle, I'll admit. You've been entrusted with a great many confidences, Doctor, in your service to the detective here," King taunted. "Have you any of which you care to unburden yourself? Or you, Mr. Sherlock Holmes? Hypnotic suggestion works on the strong-willed as well as the weak. Oftentimes more so."

"Sorry. No polished teaspoons here," I countered, carefully serene.

King shot me a surprised look, a clumsy cover for his outrage and having been bested, in part, by something so plain as that. And with that, he would say no more to us for the remainder of our short journey. Instead, he sat, eyes shut, in the swaying carriage, hissing and muttering under his breath.

We disembarked to find ourselves battling a riotous crowd. A collision between a brewer's wagon and a furniture van was causing chaos in the street. Our attentions were engaged elsewhere for a fraction of a second, and when we turned back to King? He was gone. The police handcuffs lay open and empty on the seat where he had sat but an instant before.

SETTING ASIDE THE CLOAK
OF JUSTICE

CHAPTER 18

"**Q**uick, man!" Police whistles sounded, and Watson and I darted through the crowd.

But it was to no avail. King had slipped into the pandemonium. Lestrade was swearing.

"Now we know why he confessed," he said.

"We will find him, Lestrade," I assured. "Watson—"

"Mrs. Jones?" he finished, throwing out his hand and whistling sharply for a cab.

"And I'll set men to hunting our fugitive," Lestrade vowed.

Watson and I piled into a hansom cab and I cried, "Number 26 Hill Street, quick as you can."

King had set plans within plans. Clenching my fists, I bemoaned our failure, "And in a puff of smoke and flash of a mirror, the magician disappeared."

Mrs. Jones was not at home. The maid hadn't any idea of when the lady of the house had left. She remembered Simmons coming by. His message lay untouched on an entryway table. I added my own note to the pile, and Watson and I moved on.

A bold and foolish thought struck my brain as our cab turned toward Baker Street. I rapped the roof, and the driver's face looked down through the flap.

"Never mind Baker Street," I cried and gave King's address in substitution.

"He would never——!" Watson breathed his disbelief.

"Which is why we must try," I countered, stone-faced above my pounding heart.

King's house was closed and quiet.

"He has fled." Watson shook his head.

I held up a finger for silence. "If that is indeed the case, then we have unexpected opportunity afforded us. Come, Watson."

In the growing darkness of the coming evening, we slipped into a nearby alley. I whispered, "If King can be cavalier with the law, I find no objection in following suit myself. But I confess I have not come armed for this adventure."

"Neither have I, but I am with you, through and through, old man," Watson said. "Though, if Lestrade has to clap irons on us at day's end rather than on the true villain, I will not easily live down the shame of it."

I smiled, and carefully, we made our way unseen into the area.

Tense minutes later, we had set aside the cloak of justice to become burglars. Watson was correct. King had not returned home after escaping from the custody of the police. A wealth of evidence lay around us, however. The ghosts of the false names and false lives King had previously adopted in Vienna, Paris, Munich, and Rome rose up in the form of papers and bank accounts, articles and monographs, and outdated lecture notes. From what I could see here, I expected that 221B Baker Street would soon receive a reply to my telegrams from the day before confirming that King had begun to forward his assets, care of a future self named Grant.

"Holmes!" Watson's hissed alert gained my attention, and I turned from the pilfered desk contents. My friend held in his hand a small piece of paper. A telegram.

"I found this in the next room over," he explained. I bent close to read it.

"Come, Watson, we have not a moment to lose!" I cried.

Outside, Watson raised his hand for a cab.

"We'll use the Underground. Simmons lives close to Southfields," I said, beckoning.

I quickened my pace only to find that I hurried alone. I turned to look for my companion. Watson was speaking to a boy some steps back. I waited, impatient, while the two gestured through their brief conversation. With a nod of thanks and the offering up of a coin, Watson concluded their business and hurried to catch me up.

"We cannot take the train," he huffed, again raising his hand for a cab.

"Who was that?"

"I thought him one of your boys," Watson replied.

I frowned.

"He said the line is blocked, and we must stick to the streets if we are to get there in time," my friend insisted, still looking 'round for a cab.

My frown deepened. "Telling him our business, Watson—"

"I did not tell him. He knew!" Watson cried, looking back to where the youth lounged in the shadows.

A shiver touched my spine, and I moved forward, intent on seeing this strangeness through. My path was blocked by a cab swinging toward the kerb. When I craned my neck to espy the youth, he had gone.

"We're taking the train." I was firm. With a waved apology to the grumbling cabman, I set off for the nearest station. It was efficient. It was logical. It was against anything that unknown boy had said. For I could not trust his word. Who was he? How would he know where we were going and why?

"Get there in time," I muttered.

"What?"

"Nothing," I said, settling our fare and embarking on the train.

Our journey was halted prematurely. Our conveyance slowed, then slowed some more, before finally coming to a stop. Word was passed around. Some emergency on the line ahead. We were delayed.

We had no choice but to bet on the duration of this wait or disembark and retrace our steps. We chose the latter. The hour was growing late and the traffic thin when we crossed Putney Bridge at long last.

In the end, we were mere minutes too late.

"IT WAS POISON"

CHAPTER 19

Rushing up the steps of Simmons' home, we rang and were met with no response whatsoever. We rang again.

"Curse it, man, answer!" I said to no one in particular. I fished in my pockets for my lockpicks. What fortune that I should have thought to have them on me today, though in truth, I had half expected that we should have had to surprise King at one point or another.

'You know justice, Mr. Holmes.' The words rang oddly in my head.

Did I, Simmons? Did I?

We entered and found King's hat and coat on a peg in the entryway. Silently I beckoned Watson forward, but in the quiet home, I already knew there was no need for such caution. Opening the door to the next room, we found Simmons and King sitting at a table. Both were dead.

"It is poison," I said to Watson, arresting him

in the motion of inspecting the bottle and two glasses which sat on the table between the two men. "Come, let us call for the assistance of someone with a little more authority than ourselves."

Lestrade did not question our presence within Simmons' home. "Funny, him leaving the door unlocked and all," was all he said of it and then stepped aside to let his men do their work. Simmons had kept his note to us upon his person. Perhaps he had feared treachery from King to the very end and thought it safest. Or, perhaps, he merely wished it to be a more personable discovery. The tone of it was very cordial, after all.

It was as Watson and I had feared. Simmons' message to King had summoned the misguided magician to his doorstep under the promise of clemency and assistance. The blackmailer had become the blackmailed, with Simmons threatening—falsely—that he had evidence aplenty that would ensure that King was hanged if the man so much as made any further efforts against Simmons or his flock. In exchange for this truce, he would help King escape and say nary a word of it to another living soul. Simmons had chosen to share in the poisoned brandy, proof that he was not hiding a dagger or other betrayal.

Simmons' lone servant we found cowering in a closeted space, pistol at the ready per his master's orders, should the plan go wholly wrong. He confirmed the statement made in Simmons' note. King was not to leave Simmons' house alive.

"If not me, if not her, then it is someone else. Some other Mr. James or Mr. Henry. Another Miss Overweg," Simmons' note went on to say. "Someone must stop him. Someone who can match him trick for trick must put an end to his endless and terrible terrors. And if the cost of this victory over evil be my death, then I forfeit myself most readily. My passing will hold no horror for me to know that I have rid the world of such a villain."

NO APOLOGIES NECESSARY

CHAPTER 20

I was wrong in that my investigation into King's finances did not prompt as quick a response as hoped. I had to wait four more days before my overtures to various authorities produced any fruit. In the end, it was confirmed that Mr. William Grant had already begun to replace Mr. Frederick King in various circles—most particularly those which could be verified by his bank.

In the meantime, a brief worrying line of investigation was taken up by the police, wherein the question of Simmons potentially being the puppet master was given full consideration. Had King been set up for a fall? Were these horrid events meant to drive Mrs. Jones back to Simmons' waiting arms?

Lestrade was thorough and he was practical. Control over a person such as King—and it was agreed that he was the mesmerist in this instance

—would have left a trail, some sort of evidence. We found none.

The evidence from King, however, corroborated with his own statement during his arrest, showed more and more the machinations of a twisted and malevolent mind. It was established that King had employed Mr. James in a good deal of clandestine activities. Evidence of some half a dozen burglaries more could be gleaned from their private papers. Two had been against the members of Simmons' own order so that King might work his game against them. Mr. James had, also, been employed in the addressing of the envelopes used to send Mrs. Jones the vexing diary pages.

To that end, Mrs. Jones would not long have been alone in her distress. Tidy collections of secrets waited for unleashing onto unsuspecting victims. From the contents of his study, it was apparent that King had years of entertainment stacked up for his amusement and had bundled the majority with the idea of taking it with him when he fled to the Continent.

Detective Inspector Lestrade was able to keep most of the tragedy from the papers long enough to allow my brother's connections a fair bit of progress in tracking Mrs. Jones' whereabouts. In the end, we were informed that she had been bundled off to Berlin under the care of a trio paid in advance by King. Two men and a woman. Theosophists all.

There the trail ran cold. This detail itched in my companion's brain, rendering my normally even-tempered Watson morose and biting for days on end.

"We sit here, Holmes, reading through the papers of some dominating egoist, connecting threads which no longer matter. While Mrs. Jones is out there somewhere and at the mercy of goodness knows what," he complained.

From my desk, I cast a phlegmatic eye his way. "You've my blessing to go after her, Watson. My work is here. I have no less than a dozen cases pressing for my immediate attention, the aftereffects of the Simmons case are a mess, and my brother has reassured me that his men will see that no harm comes to the wayward Mrs. Jones. We still have no proof that she was an unwilling participant in this whole affair."

"No proof. No proof!" Watson bristled. "You're swimming in the proof, Holmes. I see it there all over the desk. Boxes and boxes of it. King was a blackguard. A puppeteer pulling everyone's strings."

"Lestrade and his ilk have made their conclusions. Let me pursue mine. At present, what we have is King's word against Simmons'—in the form of what documentation the two men left behind. The key witness is gone abroad, with her last known associates being people friendly to King. Add to that the fact that the case against King hinges on his reported ability to place people in a mental state where they were willing to set down written confessions and ideas, in their own hand, which would be damaging to their own reputations."

"A mess," Watson agreed at last. "But one which is over and done and still you press at it as though new meaning may yet be derived. Besides, you, me, and Lestrade had that man's confession verbatim."

"Moments before his extraordinary and convenient escape from police custody," I grimaced.

To that, Watson gave no rejoinder.

"It may be that we never recover Mrs. Jones," I cautioned, turning back to my work. "Which is why I am more useful here than tramping about the continent looking for a woman who, all signs point to, is not in active danger."

A ring at the front bell had Watson craning his neck in surprise. I hardly turned. It was a visit which I had been expecting. Moments later, Mr. Thomas Carter stood within our sitting room looking both striking and distinctly uncomfortable.

"I believe I owe you an apology, Mr. Holmes," he began.

"Have a seat, Mr. Carter." I gestured. "No apologies necessary."

"Still, I ought not have lumped you in with King and his type," Carter said. "That's where I had you, in with the likes of him."

He shook his head. "At least until you wrote to me. What happened to James shook me. Then I heard of what occurred between King and that man Simmons. Bless him. Bless Simmons for doing what none of us could have dared to do. I know it's not right to celebrate a man's death. But King was no man, he was a monster. A monster who I would not let from my life, what with what he gave me. Now, this isn't something the police will have from me, is it, Mr. Holmes?"

I shook my head. "In full honesty, I simply wanted to hear of King's influential methods from anyone willing to speak on it."

"My son," Carter began. His fingers played with a coin on his watch chain, and his eyes grew distant. "King would tell me about my son, Mr. Holmes, through the powers he proclaimed. Just enough to hold my interest, mind you. I'd have called him a charlatan and chased him out of my life, but he told me what I wanted to hear. For a price, of course. And right or false, I wanted to hear what he had to say. The others of King's powers were of a . . . Let's just say he held a certain mental control over people. I never let him do that with me, so far as I could tell. I knew what he did to James. I— I helped sometimes. Payment for what King could tell me of my son. He had me, he did. Just like the others. Not my limbs. Not my mind. But he had me just the same."

Thanking us for the privilege of having been allowed to speak his mind on the King matter, Carter left.

I eyed Watson, who appeared thoughtful. "You

brought up the son on purpose at dinner. It was a test for King as much as a demonstration."

Smiling, I said, "Now why would I stoop to such a thing as that? I merely noted the coin and its bright blue scrap of ribbon upon the man's chain and began to employ my methods. The Shipwrecked Mariners Society has any number of supporters, of course, and I had to account for other aspects of the gentleman if I were to have anything worth saying at all."

A tumult on the stairs drew our attention back to the door. We rose, expectant. It was not Mr. Carter returned but rather Mr. Daniel Turner of the Society of Universal Energies.

I blanched, and he pursed his lips in agreement over my reaction. "It does not come as a surprise to you, Mr. Holmes, that I am not happy. I have followed the story in the papers, and I have put two and two together. Your questions to me concerning Mr. Frederick King, Mr. Percy Simmons, and everyone else in his set. Your interest in my little group and its creeds.

"Our beliefs are not your plaything, Mr. Holmes. My altruism is not to have been your clever way of getting information from an otherwise closed circle. The Society of Universal Energies is neither a gossip circle nor a gentlemen's club. Consider your application denied. You will not be hearing further from me. Shameful, sir."

Turning, he jammed his hat upon his head, nodded curtly to Watson, and left.

Dumbfounded, I stared at the closed door.

" 'Ah, Watson, but what if there were methods for a criminal's bag other than the base and palpable gun, lockpick, or knife?' " Watson threw an approximation of my words back at me with a sly sideways glance.

I hardly heard Watson's inquiry, his astute implication, through the roaring rush of my disappointment. Hope extinguished itself, and I, again, felt yawning, empty space open up beneath me. I looked to Watson, waiting on a response from his challenge, and forced my nerves back into steadiness through sheer will and a touch of indignation that my genuine interest should be so discredited. I sniffed and waved a dismissive hand. "Mr. Turner is more informative than a library. Theirs is not a common knowledge."

"Theirs is not an open index of information," Watson added, his keen gaze telling me that he was not altogether mollified.

"Indeed." I moved on, adding, "And did I not say from the first, Watson: where your name inspires confidence, friendships, and open doors, mine tends to provoke enmity."

MOUNTAINS AND CLIFFS

CHAPTER 21

I sat upon a high mountain. The apex of the world, from there I imagined I could see everything. Every lie being told. Every promise being kept. Every honour upheld. Every desperate scramble for the simple means to get by. Every gravestone. Every hearthside.

I had sought peace but had been answered with a roar and a rush, a shimmering waterfall instead of a placid lake. Perhaps there was no calm to be had for humanity. Perhaps even the gravestones trembled and danced, the dead restless through all time. Moriarty's scream unending in my ears.

I stood in the ceremonial hall of Simmons' order. A sword lay across my neck though I, myself, was hooded so that I could not see the wielder. The sword pressed my flesh—vital promise—then lifted—clemency.

A new life granted.

The falls tumbled at my feet, Moriarty shouting his curses from the base of its cruel depths. I turned. I walked away. I was being given the chance at anything I wanted, any life, any name. My brother would see that I was comfortable, possibly even useful. I could serve as spy or expatriate, scholar or monk. I would not go back. I dare not go back and face, again, the painful drudgery of the ordinary everyday, the whirring of my brain like some gear in a clock as I awaited— hoped for!—some terrible tragedy to cross my path so that I might feel useful and good.

The falls tumbled at my feet, and I was unable to walk away. Moriarty beckoned with tantalizing promise—a case, an adventure, unlike any other I had faced . . .

"Holmes. Sherlock!" Watson stood over me, his face lined with worry. "I have been calling you for some minutes."

I sat up, disoriented, and discovered that I lay, not on the couch of our sitting room, but rather on the floor at its feet. A haphazard chalk circle surrounded me. My fingertips were dusted with it. They were cold. Every bit of me was cold. Blinking, I crawled into the cane chair and reached for my tobacco.

"Was I yelling?"

"No."

"Was I disturbing you?"

"Outside of you not waking at my call? No."

"Then whatever is the problem, man!" I cried.

Without a word, Watson went over to the desk and returned with my calendar. "This is the problem, Holmes. Your inability to stop and take any time for yourself. And when you do sit still, it is to lose yourself in—in whatever this is! You may as well be on the moon."

"I see I am annoying you with my explorations," I said archly. "I'll take care to perform such practices in my room."

Exasperated, Watson paced the floor. That he kept his eye on me the whole time was telling. It was as if he expected at any moment that I should be spirited off. He paused at the table to pick up a small yellow slip.

"Mrs. Jones has been found," he said, then handed me the telegram. "I had a call to your brother about it, in fact. Mrs. Jones hadn't any explanation of how she got to where she was, and she is unhealthy but unharmed. The word your brother used was 'faded.' She has a sister who is to collect and take her somewhere to let her mind settle. Somewhere far from anything her recent life has touched.

"Which brings me to you," Watson concluded. "And how you are allowing yourself to fade. What is this nonsense? Is it the Simmons and King case? That concluded weeks ago. There is nothing more for you to discover there, Holmes."

I opened my mouth to speak, found that I

could not say the words, and so said nothing. He waited.

At length I said, "There is something exceptionally relieving in the act of being able to point at this or that and say 'It is evil!' It removes us from a position of responsibility whether it be in equity, equality, means, or meanness. Look at our philanthropists. Man made better through temperance, through reading, through church. If these well-meaning people could but follow the average pickpocket through their week—a day, even—sup at his table and sleep against the wall of his room, they might know the hard scrabble and desperation that drives a man to such a livelihood. Evil. Bah. Jealousy, we have. Passion and greed and lust and wrath, envy and pride—we unmistakably have. There is little evil in this world that may be ascribed to anything other than man and his littleness of heart.

"A theory, Watson. A theology, if you will.

"I wanted to confirm that. When Simmons stood on that spot there and talked of good and evil, I wanted to follow that thread. For myself. A fair part of me dreaded the answer. For to identify evil as existing or not existing would place me upon the board myself, set myself open to judgment. I live. I try to live well."

"And live well you do, Holmes!" he cried. I blanched.

"I am lesser when I ignore my part in the role I have chosen, where my name sits upon the balance sheet of good and evil," I said. "I killed Moriarty. I did it. I would do it again, given the choice."

"Self-defence."

I flashed a quick, barren smile. "Were I able to look at it that way, I would not be captive within this moral and ethical dilemma. I think of Frederick King's words to us. I need a confessor."

"You need confess nothing to me," Watson replied. "But know that my ears, my heart, I am always open to hear anything you have to say."

I considered how I might explain it to him. What am I saying? I fretted. Mentally, I thrashed about in search of a place to hide, for the means to quickly and silently disavow that secret unworthiness which lurked in my heart. For Watson would not understand. If I could tell him, he would not understand.

Daring to look at him, I realized he might.

And so at last the truth poured out of me as I said, "Why did I choose this work to begin with, oh so long ago? You would likely state it, in your penetrating way, as a sense of justice blended with a certain calculated coldness. I would very much agree with that assessment. Remove one element, however. Alter any detail of my life, my moral makeup, flip a coin in the hands of fate, and I could have been Professor Moriarty instead of Sherlock Holmes. This I realized with stark clarity in the moment I went over the falls in my opponent's arms. We each believed ourself perfectly correct. Myself and my enemy, both of us have been, in our own way, perfectly content within our facts and systems. Disconnected.

"And before you say 'That's not possibly true, Holmes' . . . I went away for three years and let you believe that I was dead." The admission made me tremble, and I paused. Patiently, Watson waited for me to finish. "And when I came back, unexpectedly and with my prideful turn of drama, I didn't even think how it might have an effect on you.

"The fact remains that it struck me, very clearly, how I could have been the villain and never known it. I could have been a ruiner of lives," I concluded miserably.

Watson huffed and scowled. "What's all this matter? You aren't Moriarty. You have that strong sense of justice, as you say. And you punish yourself—more than anyone I know—in its service. It is Simmons' death which—"

"It pushes me! The work. This need!" I cried. "It is a relentless taskmaster. I crave the challenge, the labour. It completes me. Without it, who am I? Without it—"

"You are Sherlock Holmes. A master of himself. And a good-hearted friend." Watson made sure to emphasize the second, eyeing me sternly so that I could not shrink from his words. "That which would ease your conscience, the defining of good and evil, fate and destiny, does not lie with Simmons or King or Turner. They may, through their beliefs, have developed a way to explore those questions, consider possible answers. But they don't have those answers. They seek them. It is, I believe, one of the most basic tenets of their faith: the power of the mind and of the will. And I know no person with a stronger will or mind than you, Holmes."

I smiled wryly. "Watson, this smacks of a rehearsed lecture. You anticipated this outcome. You've my immense gratitude for allowing me to come to it on my own."

"The mind can, itself, be a strange, wild wilderness. And to say anything at all . . ." Watson shrugged.

". . . would have had me push back all the more. Agreed."

"A formidable brain." Watson tapped his head. "Bent to the purposes of self-preservation, it would have been a fierce opponent against any advice I could give."

"And now?"

He waited, silently throwing my question back at me.

"And now I look to my doctor for recommendation," I conceded.

Watson replied, "I would recommend to you what I would recommend to any patient experiencing what you have. Rest. Proper rest for mind and body. No work. Take yourself somewhere away from any and all places and people who would be wont to distract you from purposeful and pointed leisure."

"Would you go with me?" I asked.

Watson was nonplussed. "My dear fellow, I would follow you to the brink and back, you know that."

EPILOGUE

Were it as easy as Doctor J. Watson of 221B Baker Street prescribed.

We took ourselves off to the country for a long-delayed holiday. There amongst the late autumn foliage of harvest golds and pale yellows, my mind still dashed about in search of anything that would satisfy its energies. I allowed myself to adopt several new lines of study lest I find that I became driven to distraction—or worse. But my heart, my heart was eased for the moment.

Crime would still be there when I returned to London some weeks from now. My presence did not prevent it. Nor could I solve even a fraction of what happened within those noisome, twisting, wonderful old streets.

What I could do was what I can. What any of us can. Make the lives around us a tiny bit easier, a tiny bit brighter for our efforts. Not in grand gestures and not merely because it satisfies us. But because it is right.

Today, as on the day before, my friend and I had traipsed amongst the bouquet of hills and trees, the forests and babbling brooks which surrounded the picturesque university of whose library I was availing myself. We sat creek-side, Watson watching the water and making an occasional remark about fishing, while I pretended to read the book I had pocketed for our walk. The wind rushed over my face and slithered through my upturned collar, clearing the last of the lingering morning mist and ushering in what promised to be one of the last truly warm spells of the year.

For me, one place was as fine as another.

But there was Watson to think of. Watson and his good sense.

To my great shame, I realize now that I had only ever asked if he was game, not if he was happy. I never asked. It never occurred to me to ask. Yet through all of my selfishness, my arrogance, he has never left or abandoned me.

And now, at my weakest, he is there. He passes it off as a doctor's care and the personal knowledge gained through his own traumatic exit from India in the year his path crossed mine. Perhaps he has been partnered with me too long, and my habits of myopic self-deception have become his own. Perhaps. I see his care as stemming from the abiding love which comes from the deepest and truest friendship either of us may ever know. And that, in itself, is as clear an answer as any heart can hope.

AUTHOR NOTE

At several points in the process of writing this story, I voiced an argument to myself. It ran, more or less, along the lines of "But nobody wants to see Sherlock in such a state as this!" The characters of Sir Arthur Conan Doyle are beloved to me and to so many, how dare I take such a superhuman, a hero, and break him all to bits.

That, in and of itself, was the argument I needed to hear. The fact that mental anguish, one of the most powerful and real human experiences our minds can endure, is so often denied and hidden away . . . This was a topic worth exploring. Particularly as I saw the setup as being right *in* the original Canon.

Sherlock was dead. Doyle dropped him off a cliff and walked away. He penned a note in his calendar about it. The entry from Dec 1893 reads "killed Holmes." Public outcry and an author's later decision to do more with the character brought Holmes back for some three-dozen-odd adventures further before Doyle eventually allowed his great detective to retire in peace. The Great Hiatus, Holmes' three years away living under an alias, Doyle's own ten-year break from the character, melts away when Sherlock pops back up in London, shocks Watson into fainting "for the first and the last time" in his life, and neatly handles what remains of the Moriarty gang, all in one exciting short story.

Too, in Canon, Sherlock Holmes is not in the habit of being cavalier with life and death. Surely the fatal struggle at Reichenbach would have left its bruises on his psyche. For me, Holmes' and Watson's buoyant attitude post-Hiatus often reads as a pointed dismissal of mental trauma. A whistling in the dark, if you will.

And so, I offer this humble proposal, a link in the chain to explain how:

"It was in the year '95 that a combination of events, into which I need not enter, caused Mr. Sherlock Holmes and myself to spend some weeks in one of our great university towns . . ."

- *The Adventure of the Three Students*, A. Conan Doyle

ACKNOWLEDGMENTS

Ask a Sherlockian what their favourite Canon story is, and you'll get one of sixty answers. Mine has, for a very long time, been "The Adventure of the Empty House" and for one simple reason: Kid-me was flying though the stories and had no idea what she'd encounter at the end of "The Final Problem." My solution? Read the next book with haste! The emotional satisfaction of Holmes' return has stayed with me to this day and, per my note above, sparked the question of what the characters themselves might have been feeling underneath all the bravado and bluster of returning to business as usual.

Many, many thanks go to my dream team of MeriLyn Oblad, Egle Zioma, and Bernard Faricy, who help make my creative conjuring something real and tangible. And, though he once dropped our beloved Sherlock Holmes off a cliffside, eternal thanks to Sir Arthur Conan Doyle for the great cast of characters who us Holmesians love so very much.

ABOUT THE AUTHOR

M. K. Wiseman has degrees in Interarts & Technology and Library & Information Studies from the University of Wisconsin-Madison. Her home office (really, it's more a nest at this point) is cluttered with the knickknacks and memorabilia of . . . (As I write this, I look around and, frankly, it's a bit undefinable.) At any rate, the mess produces books and is a fair approximation of M. K.'s regular creative state. Suffice it to say, amongst the chaos are tokens of awards her books have won, a Fellowship of little neon tetras, and a very old typewriter which sits on M. K.'s childhood writing desk and begs the next story to come forth.

Printed in the USA
CPSIA information can be obtained
at www.ICGtesting.com
LVHW061350180823
755512LV00007B/256

9 781734 464177